early years wishing well

Collected rhymes, stories, songs and information text

Journeys and transport

Author	**Editor**	**Designer**
Liz Powlay	Lesley Sudlow	Micky Pledge
Compilers	**Assistant Editor**	**Illustrations**
Stories, rhymes and information text compiled by Jackie Andrews	Saveria Mezzana	Jenny Tulip
Songs compiled by Peter Morrell	**Series Designer**	**Cover artwork**
	Anna Oliwa	Alex Ayliffe

Acknowledgement:
Qualifications and Curriculum Authority for the use of extracts from the
QCA/DfEE document *Curriculum guidance for the foundation stage*
© 2000 Qualifications and Curriculum Authority.

The publishers gratefully acknowledge permission to reproduce the following copyright material:

Jill Atkins for 'The journey of a seed' © 2002, Jill Atkins, previously unpublished; **Clive Barnwell** for 'Clip clop' © 2002, Clive Barnwell, previously unpublished; **Richard Caley** for 'Ferry, car or train?' © 2002, Richard Caley, previously unpublished; **Sue Cowling** for 'Going to school' © 2002, Sue Cowling, previously unpublished; **Susan Eames** for 'Dashing along', 'My family are travellers', 'Helpful wheels', 'Buy a ticket', 'Come along with me' and 'Stand and wait' © 2002, Susan Eames, all previously unpublished; **Barbara Garrad** for 'The ro-ro ferry' and 'How things have changed' © 2002, Barbara Garrad, both previously unpublished; **Carole Henderson-Begg** for 'Aeroplane, aeroplane' © 2002, Carole Henderson-Begg, previously unpublished; **Val Jeans-Jakobsson** for 'Going for a bike ride', 'This big ship',

'My spaceship' and 'The high fliers' © 2002, Val Jeans-Jakobsson, all previously unpublished; **Penny Kent** for 'A long car journey' © 2002, Penny Kent, previously unpublished; **Karen King** for 'The old red van' © 2002, Karen King, previously unpublished; **Patricia Leighton** for 'The holiday train' © 2002, Patricia Leighton, previously unpublished; **Catherine Morrell** for 'Postcards' © 2002, Catherine Morrell, previously unpublished; **Peter Morrell** for 'Going in a rocket' and 'Have you heard?' © 2002, Peter Morrell, both previously unpublished; **Judith Nicholls** for 'Santa's flying socks' © 2002, Judith Nicholls, previously unpublished; **Sue Nicholls** for 'Fairground drivers' © 2002, Sue Nicholls, previously unpublished; **Mandy Poots** for 'Jungle journey' © 2002, Mandy Poots, previously unpublished; **Hazel Priestley-Hobbs**

for 'Going to town' © 2002, Hazel Priestley-Hobbs, previously unpublished; **Geraldine Taylor** for 'Peter goes to the moon' © 2002, Geraldine Taylor, previously unpublished; **Celia Warren** for 'Snug inside my buggy' and 'Sleigh ride' © 2002, Celia Warren, both previously unpublished; **Stevie Ann Wilde** for 'Sabia's new outfit' © 2002, Stevie Ann Wilde, previously unpublished; **Margaret Willetts** for 'Henry goes to school' © 2002, Margaret Willetts, previously unpublished; **Brenda Williams** for 'Five little engines', 'Helicopter', 'Tomorrow's journey', 'The horse post' and 'Magic carpet' © 2002, Brenda Williams, all previously unpublished.

Every effort has been made to trace copyright holders and the publishers apologize for any inadvertent omissions.

Text © 2002 Liz Powlay
© 2002 Scholastic Ltd

Designed using Adobe Pagemaker

Published by Scholastic Ltd, Villiers House,
Clarendon Avenue, Leamington Spa, Warwickshire CV32 5PR
Visit our website at www.scholastic.co.uk
Printed by Ebenezer Baylis & Son Ltd, Worcester

1 2 3 4 5 6 7 8 9 0   2 3 4 5 6 7 8 9 0 1

Contents

Early years wishing well: Journeys and transport

Contents

Photocopiables

Wishing Well: Journeys and transport

The *Wishing Well* series is designed to help early years practitioners by suggesting exciting ways for them to provide a balanced curriculum for young children. The books contain a wealth of rhymes, stories and songs linked to a familiar theme, and also offer information text and ideas to stimulate activities which meet the requirements of the Early Learning Goals.

Themes

By using themes that are within the children's recent experience, practitioners can build upon what is already known, and learning becomes relevant, integrated and fun. Young children are always making journeys – short ones to the shops, a friend's home or their setting, and longer ones when going further afield. Through the activities suggested in this book, children can be encouraged to take a closer look at people who make journeys and ways to travel around. Some activities deal with methods of transport that are familiar favourites, such as a train ride; others introduce more unusual ideas, for example, a sleigh ride.

Using an anthology

Young children benefit from the group participation that these texts encourage, as well as from the rhyme and repetition of poems and the melody of songs. The activities will help children to think about what is read to them, encouraging them to ask questions and seek further information.

Early Learning Goals

Providing a balance of learning opportunities for children is a demanding role, and practitioners may often find that time is limited. This book is therefore organized to provide quick and easy access to a wealth of ideas and inspiration. Users can be confident that the activities closely relate to the requirements of the Early Learning Goals, with ideas for all six Areas of Learning. The ideas can be applied equally well to the documents on pre-school education published for Scotland, Wales and Northern Ireland. They are designed to appeal to a wide range of children in different types of settings, including those with special educational needs.

How to use this book

This book can be dipped into for a one-off session, or used to plan a mini topic or a whole theme. The majority of the activities encourage learning through a hands-on, play-orientated or conversational approach, as these are the ways that young children learn best. Browse through the book and select texts and activities, using the children's interests, attention span and individual learning pace as a guide. Since the activities are related to a common theme, new material from other pages can extend learning or provide opportunities for reinforcement. The activities use easily obtained, inexpensive resources, with photocopiable pages providing further resources and support.

Five little engines

(Action rhyme)

Five little engines waiting to go

(five children stand holding numbers 1 to 5)

Waiting on the line for the whistle to blow

(whistle twice)

One went to London to visit the shops

(child holding number 5 chugs away)

One went to Bristol to see the docks

(child holding number 4 chugs away)

One chugged slowly along the side

(child holding number 3 chugs slowly away)

One went quickly to see the seaside

(child holding number 2 chugs quickly away)

But the last one left is waiting for you

(child holding number 1 points to all the children)

So hold on tight for a visit to the zoo!

(rest of group hold on to number 1 and chug around)

Brenda Williams

Five little engines

Personal, social and emotional development

★ Make an engine using a large cardboard carton and add chairs for the carriage. Sing the song 'Down by the Station, Early in the Morning' from *This Little Puffin…* compiled by Elizabeth Matterson (Puffin Books).

★ Encourage the children to think of a place to go to by train. Imagine what might happen when you get there, and act it out before 'returning home'.

Communication, language and literacy

★ Make five copies of the photocopiable sheet on page 80 on to card and cut out the five engine shapes. Write a different letter of the alphabet on each engine, for example, c, a, d, g and o. Ask the children to choose an engine, say the letter on it and find something in the setting that begins with that letter.

★ Select letters of the alphabet so that you can use the engines from the previous activity to build consonant–vowel–consonant words. Invite the children to make as many words as they can. Encourage them to write the letters across the top of a piece of paper and to list the words, adding illustrations.

Mathematical development

★ Enlarge the photocopiable sheet on page 80 to A3 size and make five copies. Cut out all the engine shapes and write the numbers 1 to 5 on them. Provide old magazines, newspapers and catalogues and invite the children to look for the numbers 1 to 5. Encourage them to stick each number on to the corresponding engine.

★ Use the children's completed engines to act out the rhyme, following the instructions given in brackets.

★ Hide the engines around the setting and challenge the children to find them and to put them in number order.

Knowledge and understanding of the world

★ Use postcards, books, jigsaws and posters to find out about some of the famous sights of London such as Big Ben, St Paul's Cathedral and the River Thames.

★ Look at a map of your rail network and discover how to get to London, Bristol or the nearest seaside from the station closest to your setting.

Physical development

★ Play 'Follow-my-leader at the zoo'. The child in front should pretend to be an animal while the other children copy his or her actions and try to guess what he or she is.

Creative development

★ Give each child a copy of the photocopiable sheet on page 80 to colour in. Use different materials to make the wheels, for example, pasta circles, buttons, fruit or vegetable prints or egg-box cups.

The holiday train

Clickety-clack over the track
Clickety-clack goes the train.
Clickety-clickety-clickety-clack
We're off to the sea again.

Clickety-clack over the track
The chimneys and roofs rush by.
Clickety-clickety-clickety-clack
'Look at the fields!' we cry.

Clickety-clack over the track
We wave to the sheep and cows.
Clickety-clickety-clickety-clack
We wave to the big black crows.

Clickety-clack over the track
We look through the window and stare.
Clickety-clickety-clickety-clack
How long until we're there?

Clickety-clack over the track
Hurrah! We can see the sea!
Click-ety... click-ety... cli-ck-ety... clack
Click.. click..

Wheeeeee.

Patricia Leighton

The holiday train

Personal, social and emotional development

★ Make a train with one chair for the engine and five pairs of chairs for the carriages. Mark a dice +1 four times and −1 twice. Play a 'Holiday train' game, inviting the children to take turns and work together as the passengers to fill the train, by rolling the dice and adding or taking away 'passengers' until the train is full.

Communication, language and literacy

★ Make name trains. Copy the photocopiable sheet on page 81 for each child so that they have as many carriages are there are letters in their name. Write the child's name in full on the engine and the letters of their name on the carriage doors. Can they arrange the carriages in the correct order to form their name?
★ Read the book *The Train Ride* by June Crebbin and Stephen Lambert (Walker Books) to the children. Help them to appreciate the changing views from a train window.

Mathematical development

★ Using the photocopiable sheet on page 81, make copies of one engine and four carriages, numbering the doors from 1 to 5. Ask each child to stick their train in order along the tracks made in 'Physical development'.
★ Make copies of the photocopiable sheet on page 81 so that each child has four engines and eight passengers cut out. Roll the dice

(made in 'Personal, social and emotional development') and encourage the children to add or take away passengers, placing them in the carriage windows. The first child to fill their train with eight passengers is the winner.

Knowledge and understanding of the world

★ Take the children on a train ride (under-fives travel free). Make a 'From the window I can see...' sheet of things to spot on the journey.
★ Ask the children to bring in different types of trains and tracks, such as push-along and wind-up, and find out how they move.

Physical development

★ Invite the children to make a train track using glue, Art Straws, matchsticks and lolly sticks to run along a long piece of paper.
★ Make a copy of the photocopiable sheet on page 81 on to card for each child. Cut out the carriages and stick them on to pieces of thick card. Show the children how to make a rubbing using paper and the flat side of a wax crayon.

Creative development

★ Say the rhyme with the children, using wooden instruments to mark the pattern of the repeating 'clickety-clack' lines.
★ Ask each child to paint a picture of a place that they would like to go to on holiday. Cover the pictures with cling film and add a black frame to make a window. Display them in a line, to look like carriage windows.

A long car journey

We're off to see our granny.
We're sitting in the car
driving down the motorway.
Is it very far?

Are we nearly there yet?
Are we nearly there?
Look! Some old aeroplanes!
Where, where, where?

We've listened to our music tapes.
We've played 'I spy'.
We've stopped for a drink and snack
and found some things to buy.

Are we nearly there yet?
Are we nearly there?
Look! A suspension bridge!
Where, where, where?

It seems a long way now,
such a long way.
We're getting very wriggly.
We want to stop and play.

Oh, we're nearly there now!
Yes, we're nearly there!
Look, there's our granny's house!
Where, where?
                    There!

Penny Kent

Early years wishing well: Journeys and transport

A long car journey

Personal, social and emotional development

★ Invite a representative of the local road safety unit to visit your setting to talk about the importance of always wearing seat belts when in a car, and the need to sit still and not distract the driver. Provide supporting literature for parents and carers.

★ Talk to the children about what they do on a long journey, for example, the games that they play, the snacks that they eat, the tapes that they listen to and so on.

Communication, language and literacy

★ Play different versions of 'I spy' with the children, for example, colours, initial sounds or shapes.

★ Read *Mr Gumpy's Motor Car* by John Burningham (Puffin Books) to the children.

★ Look at pictures of road signs and other information signs, and talk with the group about what they tell us. Invite the children to design some of their own signs for different areas in your setting.

Mathematical development

★ Ask the children to suggest what makes a destination seem 'near' or 'far away'. Talk about the difference in time that it takes to walk somewhere and to drive there.

★ Draw two large concentric circles on a sheet of paper. Label them 'near' and 'far'. Ask the children to draw a picture of a relative who lives near to them and of one who lives far away, and then encourage them to place the pictures in the correct circles.

Knowledge and understanding of the world

★ Look at a road atlas and ask the children to find the motorways marked in blue. Show them how the service areas are marked with an 'S'. Talk about what can be found there, such as petrol, toilets, food outlets and shops.

★ Help the children to use a simple paint package, for example, *Splosh!* (Kudlian), on the computer, encouraging them to draw a car, colour it in and print it out.

Physical development

★ Using posters and books for inspiration, make suspension bridges from paper, card, tape and Art Straws which could support the weight of a toy car.

★ Listen to a tape of finger rhymes and encourage the children to learn the actions that could be used on a long car journey.

Creative development

★ Help the children to draw and cut out two small car shapes from card. Glue them on either side of the length of a cork, pushing a drawing pin into the underneath of the cork. Ask the children to paint a twisty road and scenery on a piece of paper. Challenge them to 'drive' the cork car along the road using a magnet under the piece of paper.

Helicopter

Helicopter
Jelicopter
Flying near the sea

Helicopter
Jelicopter
Buzzing like a bee

Helicopter
Jelicopter
Going home for tea

Helicopter
Jelicopter
Don't you land on me!

Brenda Williams

Early years wishing well: Journeys and transport

Helicopter

Personal, social and emotional development

★ Talk about what we might hear, see and think about while flying in a helicopter. Write the children's phrases on a helicopter-shaped piece of paper.

★ Find out about different types of rescue helicopters, such as air ambulance or sea rescue.

Communication, language and literacy

★ Look at information books to find out about the special things that helicopters can do, including vertical take off and landing. Suggest to the children that you make a group book, using their illustrations and adding simple text, for example, 'Helicopters can turn around in circles'.

★ Draw a large 'H' on a piece of paper to look like a helicopter landing pad. Invite the children to use brightly-coloured marker pens to draw 'H's parallel with the original lines to make a giant rainbow 'H'.

Mathematical development

★ Invite the children to count out five helicopters, for example, toy ones or pictures on card. See how many ways they can find of arranging them on a helicopter landing pad marked into two sections – for example, two on one side and three on the other, or one on one side and four on the other.

★ Make 'jelicopters' with jelly and apples. Encourage the children to carefully measure

out the water and fill small, clean fromage-frais pots with jelly. Time how long it takes for the jelly to set. Cut rectangles of apple for the rotor blades.

Knowledge and understanding of the world

★ Find out about bees, for example, the different types, their life cycle, how they feed, the different places that they live in, the nests that they build and how they make honey. Make model bees from play dough and display them with the children's paintings, books and other resources, such as beeswax products and honey.

★ Invite the children to watch sycamore seeds fly down to the ground, turning like the blades on a helicopter.

Physical development

★ Ask the children to cut out pictures from magazines to make two collages, one showing things that would be small enough to land on the children and the other showing things that would be too big.

★ Ask the children to use different types of construction toys to build helicopters, a helicopter landing area and control tower.

Creative development

★ Dance to *Flight of the Bumblebee* (Nicolai Rimsky-Korsakov) and invite the children to pretend to be bees and helicopters flying through the air.

Going for a bike ride

(Action rhyme)

Get on your bike and off we'll go.
First it's hard and we shall be slow. *(rotate bent arms slowly)*

Turn left now – give a signal clear.
Round the corner, steady as you steer. *(put out left hand)*

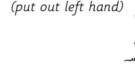

Right turn now. Stop. Look around.
Check with your eyes and listen for a sound. *(put out right hand)*

Now all's clear and it's safe to go,
But don't rush, be safe and slow. *('pedal' slowly again)*

The hill is empty so pedal down
Fast and smooth towards the town. *('pedal' fast)*

Back down the hill, right from the top,
Squeeze the brakes and then you'll stop. *(clench fists for 'brakes')*

Oh, there is just one more thing.
Ring your bell with a '**ting-a-ling-ling!**' *('ring bell')*

Val Jeans-Jakobsson

Early years wishing well: Journeys and transport

Going for a bike ride

Personal, social and emotional development

★ Talk with the children about the safety aspects of wearing helmets and protective clothing when riding bicycles.

★ Play 'Follow-my-leader' on bikes with two or three children, riding at different speeds, making hand signals before turning and using the brakes to stop.

★ Sit in a circle and gently pass a 'squeeze' around from hand to hand. Then pass a bicycle bell around without making a noise.

Communication, language and literacy

★ Using words such as 'first', 'next', 'then' and 'after', ask the children to think about and then describe how to get on a bike and ride it.

★ Read the story of *Mrs Armitage on Wheels* by Quentin Blake (Red Fox) to the children, describing a bike with lots of 'extras'. Ask the children to draw a special 'extras' bike of their own and add labels for the different parts.

★ Create a story of a bike ride with the children, perhaps a bike that has a mind of its own, or a journey around the park.

Mathematical development

★ Help the children to paint their hands, print them and label them right and left.

★ Ask the children to roll long, thin sausages from play dough and curve them around to make different-sized wheels. Try making wheels of different thicknesses.

Knowledge and understanding of the world

★ Display a selection of bike bells and hooters on a table. Let the children investigate the noises that they make. Record the sounds on to tape. Play the tape and invite the children to find the matching items.

★ Ask at a cycle shop for pieces of old tyre showing different treads. Place them on a table with hand lenses, paper and paint for the children to look at and print with.

Physical development

★ Use different-coloured paints to draw two concentric circles on to circular paper to represent a wheel and tyre. Add coloured spokes in the centre of the wheel. Give the children different-sized brushes and paper to experiment with.

★ Draw different roadways on the ground for the children to ride along. Provide opportunities to turn left and right and learn how to stop.

Creative development

★ Make a bike mobile. Invite the children to bring in bike-related items such as pictures, bells, pedals, tyres and clothing to hang from an old bike wheel.

★ Make bike-wheel snacks with the children. Cut cheese slices into discs using a round biscuit cutter. Place each disc on top of a round cracker, make the spokes with strips of carrot and put a raisin in the centre.

This big ship

(Action rhyme)

This big ship slides away from the quay
Turn the wheel and head for the sea.   *(turn 'wheel')*
It's loaded with people and now we'll ride,
Across the sea to the other side.

This sailing boat goes fast through the spray
Lean out to balance it on its way.   *(lean to one side, holding 'rope')*
Hold on tight with the wind in your face!
Keep up this speed and we'll win the race.

This rowing boat is steady and slow
Pull the oars to make it go.   *(clench fists and 'row')*
Get to the harbour and catch the tide,
One more pull and we're safely inside.

This small canoe is just my size.
Twist the paddle and see how it flies!   *(rotate arms with 'paddle')*
Sit up straight and off we dash
If you wobble about you'll fall in – SPLASH!   *(wobble and fall 'in')*

Val Jeans-Jakobsson

Early years wishing well: Journeys and transport

This big ship

Personal, social and emotional development

★ Read *Noah's Ark* (*Usborne Bible Tales* series, Usborne Publishing) to the children and talk about the Ark being full of animals and people and why God sent the flood. Help the children to act out the story using simple masks or face-paints. Ensure that everyone has a role.

Communication, language and literacy

★ Learn the words and actions to sea-related playground games such as 'A Sailor Went to Sea, Sea, Sea' or 'The Big Ship Sails Through the Alley, Alley O' from *This Little Puffin…* compiled by Elizabeth Matterson (Puffin Books).
★ Look at an information book about boats with the children. Introduce them to new boat-related vocabulary such as sail, mast, oars, paddles, port, stern, harbour and docks.

Mathematical development

★ Draw different-sized simple boat shapes on the ground. Ask the children to estimate how many children will fit inside each one before trying and counting.
★ Make a copy of the photocopiable sheet on page 82 and play a shape-recognition game with the children. Mark a dice with a square, rectangle, circle, triangle, splash pattern (miss a turn) and cloud face blowing wind (roll again). Ask each child to colour in the part of their ship that corresponds to the shape that they roll.

Knowledge and understanding of the world

★ Challenge the children to find out which materials make the best boats. Provide recyclable materials such as plastic tubs, foil, wood, card, paper, fabric, string, glue and tape.
★ Encourage the children to find different ways to make their boats move using the materials above, for example, pushing, pulling with string attached or making a sail to blow into.

Physical development

★ Invite the children to mix together blue paint, water and cellulose paste powder to make a thick mixture. Place it on a tray and draw splash patterns in it. Take a print by placing a piece of paper on top and pressing down gently. For the spray, sprinkle the print with salt flakes while wet.
★ Encourage the children to follow instructions in a simple craft book to make their own boats.

Creative development

★ Place a wobble man on the splash print (see 'Physical development' above). Pour plaster of Paris into half eggshells that have been thoroughly cleaned, leave to set and remove the shell. Add a body and head from a tube of card slid over the plaster egg and stick on collage features.
★ Invite the children to sponge-print a picture of a ship. When this is dry, add waves from strips of torn tissue paper.

My spaceship

'Goodnight,' says Mum, 'here's your Ted,
Sleep well now!' as she tucks me in bed.

But when it is dark and it's late at night,
My bed is a spaceship – we're off on a flight!

Then we can fly to a different place,
Shooting along through starlit space.

We've been to the desert – a hot dry land,
Palm trees, pyramids and burning sand.

We've been to the Arctic's icy snows,
Polar bears, icebergs and freezing toes!

We've been to the jungle – hot and wet,
Monkeys, snakes and parrots we met.

But every morning I'm back with Ted,
Waking up in my cosy bed.

Val Jeans-Jakobsson

Early years wishing well: Journeys and transport

My spaceship

Personal, social and emotional development

★ Show the children photographs of people, homes, transport and landscapes in this country and in the desert. Compare their lives with those of desert families.

★ In a quiet corner, make a spaceship bedroom role-play area where the children can go and dream of adventures. Include a bed, quilt, slippers and books to stimulate the imagination, and a teddy.

Communication, language and literacy

★ Talk to the children about other places that the spaceship bed in the rhyme could visit. Make up and type new verses for the rhyme, then print them out. Invite the children to illustrate the verses and display them in the shape of a spaceship.

★ Sing 'There were five in the bed' (see 'Mathematical development'). Ask the children to think of a journey for each teddy and record it through drawings and words on to a thought bubble. Mount the drawings above a row of five toys in a bed.

Mathematical development

★ Adapt the traditional song 'There Were Ten in the Bed' to 'There were five in the bed and Teddy said "Let's go!". So one chose a journey and off he went'. Encourage the children to enact the counting down with cuddly toys in a bed.

★ Invite the children to cut out pictures from magazines and use them to make a night-time collage on black paper.

Knowledge and understanding of the world

★ Ask the children to help you make a miniature desert on a tray with sand, water, toy camels and trees. Provide modelling sand and encourage the children to create pyramids.

Physical development

★ Invite the children to roll several sheets of newspaper into tubes and cut them down from the top to half-way in four places to make newspaper trees. Gently pull up the centre to separate the 'palm leaves'.

★ Use brightly-coloured paints to make a handprint parrot. Make a fist print for the head and two overlapping handprints with the fingers pointing downwards for the body and tail feathers. Add a handprint on either side for the wings.

Creative development

★ Make a 'palm-tree squash picture'. Fold a piece of paper in half and open it again. Encourage the children to paint half a tree with thick paint on to one half of the piece of paper. Fold over the other half and press flat while the paint is still wet, then reopen.

★ Make ice in the shape of cubes and blocks and challenge the children to build igloos with them.

Tomorrow's journey

I've taken down the pictures
I'd pinned upon my wall,
and packed away my toys,
my bike and bouncy ball.

The cupboards have been emptied.
The carpets have been rolled.
We're leaving in the morning.
Our house has just been sold.

A huge van will be calling,
and men to load it up,
with all the furniture we own
and every plate and cup.

We'll say goodbye for ever
to this house I know so well
and leave behind an empty house,
that's really just a shell.

For all of us are leaving,
the dog, the cat, and me.
My sister, and her rabbit...
Our whole family!

When everything is loaded,
we'll travel really far,
on our journey to a new house,
all squashed into our car!

I haven't seen our new house yet,
but Mummy says it's great!
That's why I cannot sleep tonight,
I just can't wait!

Brenda Williams

Early years wishing well: Journeys and transport

Tomorrow's journey

Personal, social and emotional development

★ Place a large truck alongside a doll's house and encourage the children to role-play moving house with small-world dolls and furniture. Encourage them to share their experiences of moving house as they play.
★ Read *Moving Molly* by Shirley Hughes (Red Fox) to the children and talk with them about both the excitement and concerns when leaving your home and friends to go to a new place.

Communication, language and literacy

★ Invite two children to stand either side of an easel. Ask one child to paint a picture of a house, describing what part they are painting and the colours that they are using. The other child should follow the information given and paint a copy.
★ Invite each child to talk about what their home is like. Afterwards, ask them to describe their dream home and what would be in it.

Mathematical development

★ Give each child some paper shapes and an A3 sheet of paper. Using shape and positional language, for example, saying, 'Put the square in the middle of the paper and place the triangle above it', ask the children to follow your instructions to make a house each.
★ Go for a walk with the children along a street near your setting and look for house numbers. Back in your setting, look at the addresses on envelopes, talking about how the post is delivered by the house numbers and postcodes.

Knowledge and understanding of the world

★ Draw a house outline on a large sheet of paper and mark on the rooms. Ask the children to cut out pictures of furniture from catalogues to fill the empty house ready to move into.
★ Find out and talk about animals and their homes, such as snails and their shells.

Physical development

★ Show the children how to make rubbings of brick walls. Ask them to cut them into house shapes and to print windows and doors using paint and shape sponges.
★ Invite the children to have a 'moving-house race' in teams. They have to carry items from one side of the room to a box half-way across. When the box is full, they should push it to a new house, drawn on the floor with chalk, at the end of the room.

Creative development

★ Look at designs for 'New home' cards and ask the children to design their own.
★ Pretend to be a removal person and deliver boxes to the children filled with things needed to make a home corner. Encourage them to unpack the boxes and set up their new home.

Ferry, car or train?

I'm going on my holidays
I'm off to sunny Spain
But should I go by hydrofoil,
Ferry, car or train?

I'm going on my holidays
I'm off to sunny Spain
I think I'll take the quickest route
And fly there on a plane.

Richard Caley

Early years wishing well: Journeys and transport

Ferry, car or train?

Personal, social and emotional development

★ Have a Spanish day in your setting when you cook paella, drink fresh orange juice or iced tea, listen to Spanish music and play castanets. Look at information books about Spain with the children and learn some simple words such as 'hola' (hello), 'por favor' (please) and 'gracias' (thank you).

Communication, language and literacy

★ Contact the Spanish tourist office or local travel agent's and obtain posters advertising holidays to Spain. Look at the way that colours, pictures and wording are used to promote the country. Invite the children to design and make posters for holidays to their local area.

★ Make a consonant–vowel–consonant word-building game for the children to play. Choose words linked to holidays such as sun, hat and car, and write the letters on sun-shaped cards. Lay these on a table and ask each child to select three suns and form a word. They can keep the word if it is correct.

Mathematical development

★ Pick up a handful of small toy cars or trains and ask the children to estimate how many there are before counting them.

★ Find different routes to reach a certain place in or near your setting. Time the children using a stopwatch to find the quickest route.

Knowledge and understanding of the world

★ Make a concertina book showing the different ways that you could travel to Spain. Using information from travel brochures, work out how long it would take to get there by different methods of travel.

★ Display a large map of Spain. Ask the children to cut out photographs for different contrasting areas of Spain from holiday brochures, mount them and place them next to the map, linking each photograph to the corresponding area on the map with wool.

Physical development

★ Select holiday clothes such as a T-shirt, flippers, armbands and sun-hat and explain to the children that they are going to get dressed to go for a swim. Invite them to roll a dice in turn and to try to throw a six. The child who throws a six has to try to get dressed before a different child throws another six.

Creative development

★ Play flamenco-type music and encourage the children to dance to it following the rhythm. Invite them to make up a short repeating dance. Then ask them to play 'Follow-my-leader' to the music, taking turns to copy the dances created.

★ Make a sun mobile. Hang up a large, bright collage sun with rays with a thread through the centre, then fasten small suns to the rays with different lengths of gold thread.

Going to school

My school is in Holland
Where the land is flat.
We all cycle off to school –
Wouldn't you like that?

My school is in Africa.
There's no cycle track.
We walk miles and miles to school
Then we walk miles back!

Sue Cowling

Early years wishing well: Journeys and transport

Going to school

Personal, social and emotional development

★ Talk to the children about countries such as Africa, where it is difficult for children to go to school due to long distances, no schools or lack of money. Explain what sponsoring a child means and ask parents and carers to help your setting sponsor a child through school. Display letters and pictures that you receive.

Communication, language and literacy

★ Decide on phrases for the time line (see 'Mathematical development'), for example, 'Ben and Kathryn walk to the setting' or 'Thomas builds a tower with Raju'. Type them and print them out.

★ Add speech bubbles to the children's self-portraits (see 'Creative development'). Encourage the children to tell you what they like about the setting and how they get there. Write their suggestions in the bubbles and encourage each child to write their name underneath.

Mathematical development

★ Make a survey of how the children in the group reach your setting. Ask them to draw pictures on sticky labels, showing how they travelled, and arrange these in columns as a pictogram. Talk about the results, asking questions such as, 'How do most people make the journey?', 'Does anyone come on a bike?' and so on.

★ Help the children to take photographs of activities that happen in your setting. Arrange the photographs together in a time line showing what happens during the day.

Knowledge and understanding of the world

★ Share books about life in the other countries mentioned in the rhyme, such as *One Big Family* by Ifeoma Onyefulu (Frances Lincoln), the story of an African child and her village.

★ Show the children photographs of Holland and point out how the land is flat. Introduce the saying 'as flat as a pancake', and search for flat things around your setting.

Physical development

★ Go for a brisk walk with the children and have a picnic.

★ Take small groups of children for a bike ride along a cycle path. Talk about how to ride safely and the importance of wearing safe clothing and a helmet.

Creative development

★ Invite the children to paint large pictures of themselves. Cut them out and place them on a background that the children have painted to resemble their setting.

★ Make a 'colour walk' picture. Encourage the children to step in thick paint and walk along a long strip of wallpaper, then walk back using a different colour. Notice how the colours mix together to make new ones.

The horse post

(Action rhyme)

Galloping, galloping,
All day he rides
Through all the towns
And countryside.

Galloping, galloping,
Bringing the post,
From far and wide
And coast to coast.

Galloping, galloping,
People await,
At rich man's door,
And poor man's gate.

Galloping, galloping,
Bringing the mail,
Over the hills
And over the dale.

Galloping, galloping,
Maybe there'll be
A letter for you,
A letter for me.

Sit the children in a circle and choose one child to be the postman galloping around the outside of the circle. At some point, the postman silently drops a letter behind one of the children. At the end of the poem, the child who has the letter is the next postman.

Brenda Williams

The horse post

Personal, social and emotional development

★ Talk about the different types of letters that people write such as thank-you letters, invitations, love letters, complaints and so on. Invite the children to decorate a piece of paper and write a thank-you letter to someone who cares for them.

★ Look at a collection of old stamps. Emphasize to the children the need to treat the stamps with great care when looking at them.

Communication, language and literacy

★ Invite the children to write letters to one another, placing them in their postbags (see 'Physical development'), before delivering them to a post-box (see below).

★ Invite the children to make decorated, named post-boxes to receive their mail. Encourage the group to sort the mail and deliver it to the correct boxes.

Mathematical development

★ Hide a toy horse under a set of parcels numbered 1 to 5. Ask the children to guess which parcel it is under, giving clues such as 'higher' or 'lower'. Repeat with ten padded envelopes.

★ Encourage the children to practise counting down from ten with the song 'Ten Little Letters in a Brown Sack' from *This Little Puffin…* compiled by Elizabeth Matterson (Puffin Books).

Knowledge and understanding of the world

★ Look at photographs showing how post deliveries have changed over time. Contact your local post office for other materials.

★ Set up a post office role-play area. Introduce a different method of delivering the mail each week, working through the different ages – for example, the horse post using a hobby horse, a steam train made from a cardboard box, on foot, on a bike and in a sit-and-ride van.

Physical development

★ Give each child a copy of the photocopiable sheet on page 83 and ask them to carefully cut out the postbag. Help them to fold and glue it to make the bag. Let them add pictures of a horse and mail.

★ Sit in a circle and invite a child to be the postman. Ask them to gallop around the circle while everyone sings 'Postman's knocking rat-tat-tat (three times), he's at your door '. At the word 'door', the postman drops a letter behind a child, who picks it up and chases the postman back to the empty space. They then become the next postman.

Creative development

★ Invite the children to make a small collage horse and glue it to a lolly stick. Ask them to paint a scene from the rhyme on to card and cut a slit lengthways near the bottom. Slide in the horse and make him gallop along.

Magic carpet

Sit on the carpet
And close your eyes
For this carpet is magic
And soon we will rise.

We'll float far away
Where no one has been
To see rivers of honey
And fields of ice-cream.

Sugar-topped mountains
Blackcurrant seas
Banana-milk lakes
And chocolate trees.

Whipped cream clouds
And lemonade rain
Then we open our eyes
And are back home again.

Brenda Williams

Early years wishing well: Journeys and transport

Magic carpet

Personal, social and emotional development

★ Lay small rugs around the setting at random. Ask pairs of children to lead each other in turn, one with their eyes closed, around the rugs.

★ Play 'Musical rugs'. All the children should sit on a rug when the music stops. Remove the rugs until one tiny rug is left. Can the children find a way of getting everyone on to the rug so that no one is left off?

Communication, language and literacy

★ Provide different writing materials, including metallic gel pens. Give each child a copy of the photocopiable sheet on page 84 and invite them to complete the designs around the edge of the magic carpet.

★ Select and place into a box items that could be used in a magic-carpet story, including a tiny rug and pictures of mountains and lakes. Ask groups of children to invent a story around the items. Scribe the story, in sequence, on to a set of decorated carpets (see above) before the children illustrate it.

Mathematical development

★ Make a copy of the photocopiable sheet on page 84 and draw large shapes in the centre. Ask the children to name the shapes. Take turns to roll a dice marked with shapes and invite the children to colour in the corresponding shapes on the carpet.

★ Place five small-world figures in the middle of the decorated carpets. Ask each child to find different ways of placing them on the carpet. Introduce splitting them into two groups or three groups and count the total. What do the children discover?

★ Give each child a copy of the photocopiable sheet on page 84. Invite them to colour in the designs around the edge of the carpet as repeating patterns in two colours.

Knowledge and understanding of the world

★ Make chocolate ice-cream and note the changes that occur when cream is whipped, chocolate melted and the mixture is mixed and frozen. While eating the ice-cream, encourage the children to watch it melt and return to liquid. (Check for any food allergies or dietary requirements.)

Physical development

★ Follow a recipe for home-made still lemonade. Give the children plenty of opportunities to squeeze, grate, measure out, stir, pour and drink.

Creative development

★ Look at the patterns and colours used on a selection of small rugs. Give each child an enlarged copy of the photocopiable sheet on page 84. Encourage them to mix their own colours of paint, based on those seen in the rugs, and to try to paint patterns with them.

Dashing along

(Action rhyme)

Dashing along in a train so fast,
Train so fast, train so fast,
Dashing along in a train so fast,
Come along with us.

(arms go round and round
like wheels, close to body)

Flying high in an aeroplane,
Aeroplane, aeroplane,
Flying high in an aeroplane,
Come along with us.

(arms out sideways like plane wings)

Bouncing along in a yellow bus,
Yellow bus, yellow bus,
Bouncing along in a yellow bus,
Come along with us.

(bounce up and down on your bottom)

Rowing along in a little boat,
Little boat, little boat,
Rowing along in a little boat,
Come along with us.

(rowing actions)

Pedalling fast on our dumper trucks,
Dumper trucks, dumper trucks,
Pedalling fast on our dumper trucks,
Come along with us.

(pedal with legs)

Susan Eames

Ask the children to sit down
when acting out this rhyme.

Early years wishing well: Journeys and transport

Dashing along

Personal, social and emotional development

★ Sit the children in a circle and give each child a toy vehicle from the rhyme to hold so that there are two or three of each vehicle in the circle. Play music as the children pass the vehicles around. When the music stops, call out the name of a vehicle. Encourage the children holding this vehicle to swap places so that no one is in the same place.

Communication, language and literacy

★ When the children are confident with the rhyme and the way that the lines repeat, make up other verses based on transport not mentioned, for example, a hot-air balloon, fire engine or roller skates.

★ Arrange ten chairs to make two rows of seating similar to a train or bus and place ten children's name cards in a box. Say the rhyme, taking out two cards from the box each time that the line 'Come along with us' is said. Help the children to read their names and take a seat.

Mathematical development

★ Number the pictures made in 'Creative development', for example, 1 on the picture relating to verse one, 2 on verse two and so on. Ask the children to arrange them in the correct order, asking questions such as 'Does 2 come before or after 3?'. Hide a picture and ask, 'Which one is missing?'.

★ Ask the children to paint three aeroplanes, one above the other, on a sheet of paper. While they are painting, ask questions such as, 'Which one is high in the sky?', 'Is there one higher/lower?' and 'Which is the lowest?'.

Knowledge and understanding of the world

★ Make a small-world construction site with dumper trucks, diggers, lorries, gravel, sand and polished pebbles. Encourage the children to look at the different materials and feel them, comparing their sizes, shapes and textures as they play.

Physical development

★ Give each child a copy of the photocopiable sheet on page 85 and encourage them to copy over the pattern of movement for each form of transport.

★ Enlarge the photocopiable sheet on page 85 to A3 size. Invite the children to 'drive' over the patterns with the appropriate vehicles.

Creative development

★ Cut out from strong card simple stencils of the means of transport mentioned in the rhyme. Invite each child to dab different thick paint mixtures through the holes and carefully remove the stencil. Then ask them to make a textured picture by mixing the paint with sand, rolled oats, wall filler, wallpaper paste or soap flakes.

The high fliers

Summer-time is over,
We're heading for the sun.
Winter is coming.
Holidays are done.
Swallows race together,
Gather on the wires,
Chattering excitedly,
'We're the high fliers!
Africa is down there,
How do we know the way?
That is our big secret,
You might find out one day'.

Val Jeans-Jakobsson

The high fliers

Personal, social and emotional development

★ Make a thick-card template of the bird on the photocopiable sheet on page 86 (without the long tail). Show the children how to trace around it carefully using a white crayon on black paper. Ask them to help each other to hold the bird still while they draw around it and then to cut out the birds carefully.

★ Set up a bird-feeding area and make bird cake for the birds that stay in this country for the winter. Ask groups of children to take responsibility for checking that there is food and water each day.

Communication, language and literacy

★ Talk about migration with the children. Make a display of migrating birds gathered along a wire, 'chattering excitedly'. Paint a sky and add the bird silhouettes (see 'Personal, social and emotional development'), then stick a speech bubble for each bird. Think of comments that the birds might make about their journey and its hazards, recording them on the bubbles.

Mathematical development

★ Copy the photocopiable sheet on page 86 several times and cut out the birds, missing off the long part of the tail. Put the numbers from 1 to 5 along a washing line and ask the children to peg the correct number of birds to the line, next to the given number.

Knowledge and understanding of the world

★ Talk about how some birds need to fly off for their winter migration as the days get shorter and colder and food is scarce. Go for a walk and look for these signs around your setting, such as damp, colder air and ground, dead leaves, decaying fruit, fewer insects around and so on.

★ Look for birds outside collecting together, especially swallows on overhead wires and roof-tops, getting ready to migrate. Talk about their long journey ahead over water, deserts and mountains to reach Africa where it is warm.

Physical development

★ Give each child a number – one, two or three – and play 'Migrating birds'. Ask the children to run around, each calling out their number until all are gathered together by set in a row. Then invite them to fly off to Africa, flapping their wings, swooping over deserts and flying high over mountains.

Creative development

★ Give each child a copy of the photocopiable sheet on page 86. Invite them to make handprints for the wing feathers and use finger-paints to blend colours on the rest of the bird. Help them to cut out the bird and add a washer to the tail to make the bird balance. Make a row of swallows balancing on a length of thin dowel.

Snug inside my buggy

I'm snug inside my buggy
with its squishy-squashy seat
and when Mum's in a hurry
we go rushing down the street.

My buggy bumps and rattles
and I watch my bouncy feet;
then giggle when the wheels make
a funny little squeak.

I think the wheels are singing
as they twirl and whirl along,
so I chuckle at my buggy
and its happy little song.

Celia Warren

Early years wishing well: Journeys and transport

Snug inside my buggy

Personal, social and emotional development

★ Play some 'happy music'. Sit the children in a circle and pass around a toy that giggles when squeezed. When the music stops, invite the child holding the toy to share with the others what makes them giggle and chuckle.

★ Learn the song 'If You're Happy and You Know It' from *This Little Puffin…* compiled by Elizabeth Matterson (Puffin Books). Make up a new verse based on the activity above.

Communication, language and literacy

★ Place a variety of 'squishy-squashy' items in a bag and another set on a tray – for example, soft toys, wrapped jelly cubes, small cushion and a partly-inflated balloon. Ask a child to describe what they can feel through the bag without naming it, and encourage the others to work out what it might be.

★ Ask the children why they think Mum was in a hurry and where she might be going. Talk about times that they have gone in the buggy because it was too far to walk to where they were going or because they were tired.

Mathematical development

★ Make a 'Babies in buggies' counting book. Ask the children to think of phrases based on the rhyme, for example, 'one baby sitting in a squishy-squashy seat', 'two feet bouncing around' and so on. Write the phrases on to a page for the children to illustrate.

★ Set out different numbers of dolls and buggies and ask the children to match them. While they play, ask questions such as, 'How many dolls are left?' and 'Are there more buggies or dolls?'.

Knowledge and understanding of the world

★ Fill a box with noisy baby toys and ask the children to sort them into two hoops, those that rattle and those that squeak.

★ Look in catalogues and magazines for pictures that show different ways of transporting babies and young children between places, for example, different types of buggies, backpacks, slings and car seats.

Physical development

★ Sit on the floor and make different bouncy feet patterns, for example, bounces that are slow, fast, high, low and to the sides.

★ Using slopes, ramps and planks for bumps, make an obstacle course for the children to push a buggy and doll around, without losing the occupant!

Creative development

★ Ask the children to draw a buggy from memory and then from close observation. Compare the pictures.

★ Draw a wheel shape and mark it into sections. Fill each section with a different pattern using brightly-coloured paints. Hang the wheels up so that they whirl and twirl.

Sleigh ride

Six strong huskies
pulling the sleigh,
'Mush! Mush!'
the drivers say.

Over the snow
where wheels won't go,
'Mush! Mush!'
and we're on our way.

Celia Warren

Early years wishing well: Journeys and transport

Sleigh ride

Personal, social and emotional development

★ Look at a book such as *Arctic World* by Jen Green (Lorenz Books) and compare life for a child in the Arctic with that of the children. Look at homes, food, clothing, transport and games.

Communication, language and literacy

★ Invite the children to think of six words to describe a husky. Write them on to six small husky shapes and hang them from a large husky shape. Repeat the activity using six words to describe a sleigh.

★ Make new verses for the rhyme by asking the children to describe the noise that the sleigh and huskies might make, the coldness and the snow.

Mathematical development

★ Make up number stories with the children using cut-out paper huskies and sleighs. For example, you could start a story with 'Six huskies went over the snow, one ran home and five were left'.

★ Make six different-sized huskies from paper and ask the children to arrange them in size order.

Knowledge and understanding of the world

★ Ask the children to bring in pictures and models of sleighs, and real ones if possible.

Look together at how they have a smooth bottom and runners so that they do not sink into the snow. Challenge the children to make a model sleigh from junk and wood, and test it across a tray of compacted cornflour.

★ Look at information books about the Arctic to find out more about huskies. Use them in a display, together with the children's work and models, to show their thick coats, their colour, the environment that they live in and how they pull a sleigh.

Physical development

★ Provide the children with a range of textured objects such as cotton reels, tiny sponge pieces, toothbrushes and pan scrubs. Invite them to use these and white paint to print on to black paper to make a snow scene.

★ Fold a piece of card in half and draw a simple dog outline on to it so that the fold is the dog's back. Invite the children to cut it out carefully to make a standing 3-D dog.

Creative development

★ Use pastels to draw pictures of huskies, making short lines to represent their fur. Show the children how to blend colours together by rubbing with their fingers.

★ Mix some flour and water and a little silver powder paint together to make a smooth thick paste. Place the mixture in clean squeezable bottles and invite the children to use it to draw a 'snow' picture on to dark blue paper, basing it on the rhyme.

Henry goes to school

One day, Henry the black and white kitten saw Molly's fluffy lamb school-bag on the floor. He sniffed. *Mmmm, tuna sandwiches!* thought Henry. He crept inside the bag.

Suddenly, the top of the bag was zipped across and it was swung up into the air! The sandwich box bumped Henry's head.

'Miaow!' went Henry, and he dug his claws into the side of the bag.

Unfortunately, Molly didn't hear him. With her school-bag on her back, she set off for school with her mum.

Henry looked through a hole in the bag. He spotted the milkman putting empty bottles on his milk-float. *Chink, chink, chink.*

'Miaow!' called Henry. But the milkman didn't hear him.

Molly and her mum came to a busy road. They stopped at the kerb and waited for the crossing patrol person to stop the traffic. When it was safe, they went across the road.

'Miaow!' went Henry as they passed the crossing patrol person keeping back the traffic with her 'STOP' sign. But the crossing patrol person didn't hear him. The cars and trucks rumbled their engines impatiently.

They reached Molly's school. Molly kissed her mum goodbye, then she ran into the classroom and hung up her coat and bag on her hook.

Henry managed to push his paw through the little hole in the bag. Then he pushed his nose through. 'Miaow!' he cried. 'Miaow!'

'What was that?' asked Molly's teacher. 'It came from the coat rack.'

The children turned to look – and saw Henry's little face poking out of Molly's bag.

'Henry!' said Molly.

The other children laughed. 'It's Molly's cat, Miss!' they said. 'He's come to school!'

Molly fetched her bag and everyone crowded round to watch as she unzipped it and released Henry. He was very pleased to be free again, and didn't mind when everyone wanted to stroke him.

Their teacher found a cardboard box and put in some newspaper. She popped Henry inside. Then she phoned Molly's mum and asked her to fetch Henry.

Henry was really glad to get home again. He went straight to the place he loved best – his quiet, sunny window sill – where he stretched out and was soon fast asleep.

Margaret Willetts

Early years wishing well: Journeys and transport

Henry goes to school

Personal, social and emotional development

★ Encourage the children to talk about their pets or one that they would like to own. Invite them to bring in their pets or photographs to share with the others.

★ Bring in a cuddly toy 'pet' and name it. Ask the children to look after the pet for the day and to take it with them to their favourite places around the setting. Record the day using a camera, then mount the pictures in a book.

Communication, language and literacy

★ Encourage each child to write a sentence, or scribe one for them, relating to a photograph in the pet book (see 'Personal, social and emotional development').

★ Share the poem 'Cats Sleep Everywhere' by Eleanor Farjeon from *Poems for the Very Young* selected by Michael Rosen (Kingfisher).

★ Ask the children to think of words that rhyme with 'cat' and list them on a cat outline. Repeat using the word 'bag' and a bag outline.

Mathematical development

★ Collect together bags and small toy cats. Set out different numbers of bags and cats, then ask the children to match the cats to the bags. Ask questions such as, 'How many bags are left over?', 'How many more cats are needed?' and so on.

★ Invite each child to select a box from a range of recyclable materials, so that their puppet pet (see 'Creative development') will fit in it. Encourage them to decorate it with repeating patterns, using sponges and paint.

Knowledge and understanding of the world

★ Give the children information books and other sources of information and invite them to find out about the story of milk 'from cow to cup'.

★ Help the children to carefully pour different amounts of coloured water into a row of milk bottles. Tap them gently with wooden and metal beaters and listen to the different sounds made.

Physical development

★ Invite the children to cut along the outlines of cat shapes drawn on paper, then to print black and white patterns on to the shapes using a variety of materials, for example, sponges, bubble wrap, small plastic bricks and so on.

★ Set up roads and pavements in a large space for the children to use with sit-and-ride vehicles. Invite other children to be the crossing patrol person and children going to school. Show them how to cross the road safely.

Creative development

★ Make puppet pets using a cardboard tube as the body and pipe-cleaners as legs and tail. Ask the children to decorate them with collage materials and fasten an elastic band to the top to 'bounce' each pet along.

Jungle journey

Sitting with his dad and mum in the little red boat, Billy shivered with excitement. The trees overhanging the water made the river seem dark and scary. Slowly, their boat glided along. The air was filled with strange smells and noises. Steam rose from the water.

'Look!' said Mum. 'There's a crocodile!'

'And another!' said Dad, pointing to the river bank.

Billy's eyes opened wide when he saw them. Then he spotted a big snake dangling from the branch of a tree that was right over the boat.

'Look out!' he yelled.

All three of them ducked down in the boat.

Around the bend in the river there was a small herd of elephants. One elephant was close to the bank. As the boat drew nearer, the elephant lifted up its trunk and squirted a jet of water towards Dad, Mum and Billy. They all shrieked.

'I wonder what we'll see next,' said Billy.

Suddenly, some monkeys swung across the river on long creepers, almost hitting the boat. More monkeys scampered up into the trees. Brightly-coloured birds flew around, screeching.

Billy was enjoying every minute of their journey.

Just then the boat started to go faster in the water. They heard a rumbling in the distance, and the boat rocked and swayed in the rushing water as it dodged round the rocks in the way.

'What's that noise?' asked Billy.

'It must be the waterfall,' said Mum. 'Hold on tight!'

The river swept them along, taking the boat closer and closer and closer to the rumbling sound. Suddenly, they were on the edge of the waterfall!

'It's a long way down!' yelled Billy.

'Aaaaaggghhh!' they all screamed as the boat shot over the edge, plunged down and fell with a splash at the bottom of the fall. All three of them were soaked.

'Wow!' laughed Billy. 'That was great!'

The boat drifted to a halt at the bank, their journey over. The family clambered out with the help of the boatmen on the jetty.

'Can we do it again?' asked Billy.

Dad wiped his face with his handkerchief. 'I suppose so,' he sighed, and Billy ran ahead eagerly to join the queue again for 'Jungle Journey' – the best ride in the theme park!

Mandy Poots

Jungle journey

Personal, social and emotional development

★ Set up a role-play area based on the story. Invite the children to help make a boat from a large box, a blue-fabric river, paper leaves, rolled-paper trees and simple animal costumes. Encourage them to take turns at being the animals and the family in the boat.

Communication, language and literacy

★ Think of descriptive phrases together to display with jungle pictures made by the children, such as 'as dark as' or 'thick green leaves brushing our faces'. Write them on to green creeper-shaped pieces of paper.

★ Mount animal pictures and scribe the names of the animals, writing the initial letter in a different colour. Arrange the animals in alphabetical order along a river of paper. Add a paper boat for the children to move to a letter that you suggest.

Mathematical development

★ Draw a river on to a piece of A4 paper. Place a handful of small-world animals on the river bank. Ask the children to roll a dice and add or take away that number of animals until there are ten on the river bank.

★ Using small-world animals, trees, rocks, river and pools, develop the children's positional language by asking them to place 'the elephant next to the tree' or 'the monkey behind the rocks'.

Knowledge and understanding of the world

★ Provide bowls of water and equipment such as sprays, clean washing-up-liquid bottles, pipettes and stones. Encourage the children to investigate how to make drips, jets, squirts and splashes.

★ Help the children to make a water journey for small-world people, creating boats from wood and recyclable materials, and a river from lengths of plastic guttering materials.

Physical development

★ Make snakes by drawing spirals on to large discs of thin card. Give one to each child and invite them to decorate it with patterns before cutting along the line. Add a length of string to the centre and hang up or drape through branches.

★ Play 'Walking through the jungle', creeping through the trees and leaves. Move like different creatures in the jungle.

Creative development

★ Invite each child to make a paper-plate animal mask and to decorate it to resemble their favourite animal, for example, curled paper for a lion's mane, torn tissue for monkey fur and so on.

★ Show the children artwork by Henri Rousseau, looking closely at his portrayal of jungle foliage. Provide thick paint and sponges for the children to recreate their own jungle picture.

Peter goes to the moon

'There's no one here to play with,' said Peter. 'I want to go somewhere *exciting*…!'

Peter's best friend, Mia, had gone to Disneyland and Peter was feeling really fed up. He'd played all the games he could in the garden: he'd jumped over the muddy puddle, he'd climbed up Dad's heap of building sand and he'd raced to the old plum tree and back.

'Cheer up,' said Mum. 'I can take you on a journey around the world and up to the moon.'

'When?' said Peter.

'After dinner,' said Mum. 'You go indoors and play. I've got one or two things to do before we go…'

After dinner, Mum said, 'All aboard!'

'But that's the old *wheelbarrow*!' said Peter. Dad had used it last for the sand.

Mum had cleaned it out and put two cushions in it.

'Now it's a big ship,' she said. 'Jump in!'

Peter climbed on to the cushions and held the sides of the barrow. 'A life on the ocean waves!' sang Mum, and she rolled the wheelbarrow from side to side as she splashed it through the big puddle.

Peter held on tight and giggled. 'What next?' he said.

'Now it's a helicopter,' said Mum. 'And we're going to the jungle. Look out for wild animals!'

Peter looked down and saw his toy elephant and lion in the weedy patch at the edge of the garden.

'What next?' he asked.

'Now it's a camel in the desert,' said Mum. 'And we're going over the sand dunes. Watch out for snakes!'

Mum huffed and puffed and pushed the wheelbarrow up the sand pile and rolled it down the other side.

Peter giggled. 'What next?'

'Now it's a rocket and we're off to the moon!' said Mum. 'Close your eyes. Ten, nine, eight, seven, six, five, four, three, two, one… WHOOSH!'

Peter felt the wheelbarrow being pushed along very, very quickly and he held the sides tightly. Suddenly it stopped, and he almost fell out!

'Open your eyes,' whispered Mum. 'The rocket's landed.'

Peter opened his eyes and looked up. He was under the old plum tree and it was full of big silver paper stars. A huge yellow balloon hung from the top branch.

'That was the most exciting trip in the whole world!' said Peter, as Mum lifted him out of the wheelbarrow. 'Can we go exploring under the sea tomorrow?'

Geraldine Taylor

Early years wishing well: Journeys and transport

Peter goes to the moon

Personal, social and emotional development

★ Invite the children to talk about games that they play in the garden. Make a list and play them outside when the weather is dry. Repeat the activity with indoor games for wet days. Ask parents and carers to contribute any suggestions and send them a copy of your lists decorated with the children's drawings.

Communication, language and literacy

★ Chalk large letters on a play area and ask the children to push wheelbarrows along them to form the letters.

★ Go on an imaginary journey with the children. Add actions, for example, 'Bump up and down on a bumpy bus'.

★ Read *Whatever Next!* by Jill Murphy (Macmillan), a story about a bear who goes on an imaginary moon journey.

Mathematical development

★ Write numerals with glue, then sprinkle them with sand to make a set of feely numbers. Ask the children to close their eyes and work out what the number is through touch alone.

★ Make an A3 card copy of the photocopiable sheet on page 87 and cut it into pieces to make number jigsaws. Show the children the completed puzzles then jumble them up. Invite the children to roll a dice, find the corresponding piece and form the jigsaws again.

Knowledge and understanding of the world

★ Encourage the children to make puddles around an outdoor play area with watering cans. Invite them to drive sit-and-ride vehicles through the puddles and look at the tracks that they have made.

★ Make balloon rockets to fly across a room. Stretch a long piece of thin string between two children. Inflate a sausage-shaped balloon with a pump, leaving the pump attached, then fasten a 3cm piece of plastic drinking straw to the top of the balloon with sticky tape. Thread the balloon on to the string, remove the pump and watch the 'rocket' zoom.

Physical development

★ Place soft toys into small plastic wheelbarrows and ask the children to push them around an obstacle course, ensuring that the toys do not fall out.

★ Make sand-dune pictures. Invite the children to draw wavy lines with a glue pen to form the dunes, then to take pinches of sand to sprinkle over them.

Creative development

★ Make rockets from recycled materials such as yoghurt pots, foil pie cases and so on. Decorate with tissue paper, glitter and paint.

★ Make space costumes with silver-sprayed wellies for boots, a bucket with a large hole in the side for a helmet and fizzy-drink bottles for the air tanks.

Santa's flying socks

Santa Claus was not happy. His alarm clock had not rung, he had burned his porridge, and his favourite red socks had frozen outside on the washing line. He was very late.

'Shivering shuttlecocks!' he grumbled loudly to Robbie. 'Now WHY didn't I remember to bring those socks in last night?'

Robbie looked sorry, but robins get very hungry in winter and he was worried that Santa might forget to feed him. Luckily, Santa sprinkled some food on the window sill for him.

'Shivering shuttlecocks!' Santa muttered again as he unpegged the frozen socks. He put them down on the doorstep and paddled out to the barn in his slippers to wake the reindeer.

His much-loved reindeer, however, was tucked up in a pile of hay, shivering like a big brown jelly, with his nose pressed into a large paper tissue.

'I hab a bery bad code,' whispered the reindeer. 'I'b bery sorry, but I hab to stay in.'

'Tinkling tinseltops!' groaned Santa in dismay. 'You *have* got a bad cold. Now what am I going to do?'

He patted the reindeer, gave him some warm milk and then went back to the house.

Suddenly, Santa stopped.

'That's strange!' he thought.

The socks still stood frozen on the doorstep, but sticking up between them was a large note.

Cheer up, Santa
Please don't cry.
Just put US on –
WE can FLY!

Where had *that* come from? Robbie was chirping and hopping up and down excitedly on the enormous sack of waiting parcels.

Santa knew he had to act quickly. He slipped his feet into the frozen socks…

'Shivering shuttlecocks, *you're cold*!' he gasped.

But once his feet were inside the socks, they felt surprisingly warm. Santa just had time to grab his sack before the red socks lifted him into the air and took him way, way up over the reindeer's barn. In giant leaps they went over icy fir trees, beyond mountains and valleys, snow-covered villages and frozen lakes. Soon Santa found himself sliding down a hillside towards his first stop.

It was very early on Christmas Day when Santa finished his deliveries and headed back home. The sun was only just thinking about waking, and all the children were still fast asleep.

And no one except Robbie ever knew that *this* year Santa flew to deliver his presents on… *his two favourite red socks!*

Judith Nicholls

Early years wishing well: Journeys and transport

Santa's flying socks

Personal, social and emotional development

★ Talk with the children about how Christmas reminds us of the day that baby Jesus was born. Using information books and artefacts, find out how different countries and cultures celebrate his birth.

★ Encourage the children to find out about suitable food for birds from the RSPB (visit their website at www.rspb.org.uk). Establish a bird-feeding area outdoors.

Communication, language and literacy

★ Give each child a simple sock outline and invite them to draw pictures of where they would go if they had magic socks. Scribe their story on to a second sock to place alongside the picture sock. Create a book to share.

★ Together, make a list of words that rhyme with 'cry' and use them to make new endings to the rhyme in the story, giving Santa a reason not to cry.

Mathematical development

★ Invite the children to help you make a small-world village with houses, trees, a lake and hills. Ask them to take it in turns to be Santa and deliver presents following your directions. Introduce directional and positional language, for example, 'Go past the trees, over the hill to the second green house'.

★ Ask the children to decorate simple sock outlines with spots, stripes or patterns.

Number them from 0 to 10 and use them for number-line activities.

★ Using the numbered socks above, ask the children to add the corresponding number of tiny presents to each sock.

Knowledge and understanding of the world

★ Freeze a variety of socks, keeping one from each pair unfrozen so that the children can compare the differences in feel, texture and appearance. Provide the group with hand lenses to encourage close observation of the ice crystals.

★ Make a display of different alarm clocks.

Physical development

★ Make reindeer-shaped sandwiches. Help each child to spread cream cheese on to a slice of wholemeal bread, top it with another slice and cut the sandwich into four triangles. Decorate each with a cherry nose, raisin eyes and 'Twiglet' antlers.

Creative development

★ Collect together a variety of materials that will tinkle and twinkle when caught by a breeze. For example, you could select milk-bottle tops, foil, small metal items, bells, holographic paper, old CDs, tinsel and so on. Help the children to thread these items on to lengths of silver string, and hang them outside from a ring of wired tinsel to make 'tinkling tinseltops'.

The journey of a seed

It was autumn. A fresh wind blew through the wood, over the river, along the lane and across the fields. Brown leaves fluttered from the trees and floated to the ground.

Blow, wind, blow!

An old sycamore tree stood in the middle of a field. As the wind blew, a little sycamore seed flew off a twig and spun like a helicopter blade down, down, down.

A sheep was eating grass underneath the sycamore tree. The seed landed in the thick wool on the sheep's back.

'Baa!' bleated the sheep.

She shook herself, but the seed would not fall off. So she ran across the field to the wire fence. She rubbed her back against the fence and the sycamore seed fell to the ground.

As soon as the sheep had gone back to the green grass under the sycamore tree, a big black crow flew down and picked up the seed in his sharp beak. He flapped his wings and flew away towards the wood. He was just flying over the river when he saw another crow.

'Caw!' he called, opening his beak wide.

The sycamore seed fell from his beak. It spun round and round, down and down, and landed with a

tiny splash in the water.

Flow, river, flow!

The seed floated along in the fast-flowing water for a long time, but when the river swung round a bend, the seed was washed to the river bank. It lay there in the mud for a few weeks, as the wind grew colder and colder.

Winter came. Dark clouds covered the sky and the little seed sunk down into the mud as the first flakes began to fall.

Snow, clouds, snow!

All winter long, the sycamore seed lay asleep in the mud by the side of the river. But then it began to feel warmer and snowdrops and daffodils began to grow on the bank.

Spring had arrived. The sycamore seed began to swell. It sent little white roots down into the earth and drank the water. It sent little green shoots into the air and felt the warm sunshine.

Grow, seed, grow!

It was summer at last. The seed grew a long stalk and two green leaves.

'I'm a little tree,' it said. 'One day, I'll grow into a large tree like the one I came from.'

And it did. But not for many, many years!

Jill Atkins

Early years wishing well: Journeys and transport

The journey of a seed

Personal, social and emotional development

★ Go on an autumn walk and ask each child to find something to bring back, for example, conkers, leaves, twigs and so on. Create an autumn display or use the items in a large group autumn-walk picture.

Communication, language and literacy

★ Listen and look for the 's' and 'sh' words in the story. List the 's' words on a sycamore-seed outline and the 'sh' words on a sheep outline. Invite the children to illustrate the list.

★ Cover a board with felt and make a storyboard. Enlarge the photocopiable sheet on page 88 to A3 size. Cut out the pictures and fasten Velcro to the back of each one. Invite the children to retell the story, putting the pictures in the correct order.

★ Cut out the pictures on the photocopiable sheet on page 88 and make a 'Seed journeys' book, placing one picture to a page. Find out more about different types of seeds from information books and add this to the book.

Mathematical development

★ Using a bucket balance and toy sheep, find out how many seeds are needed to balance different sheep. Try a variety of seeds such as conkers, beans, peas and acorns.

★ Cut out a set of tree shapes from card, each a different height. Ask the children to order them by height, shortest to highest.

Knowledge and understanding of the world

★ With adult helpers, play 'Pooh sticks' with the children, watching twigs and seeds made from thin card, based on the seed on the photocopiable sheet on page 88, float along a stream or river.

★ Grow seeds that are quick to germinate, such as radish. Watch the shoot and leaves emerge, and gently tip the seeds out to find the roots.

Physical development

★ Draw outlines of sheep on to card and invite the children to cut them out. Snip pieces of wool and glue them on for the fleece. Show the children how to open and close wooden-spring clothes pegs and attach these for the legs.

★ Go for an outdoors sensory walk with the group and ask the children to find different types of seeds – for example, 'helicopters' (sycamore and lime), 'parachutes' (dandelions), 'stickers' (goosegrass), 'pods' (poppies) and 'exploders' (broom).

Creative development

★ Make a 'four seasons' group collage based on the ideas in the story sequence on the photocopiable sheet on page 88, creating a panel for each season. Integrate natural materials such as leaves, bark and seeds into the collage, and add loops to the top so that it can be hung on a wall.

The old red van

Ryan's mum and dad owned a greengrocer's called 'Bayley's'. They had a very old red van, with *Bayley's* written in old-fashioned lettering on the side, which they used to fetch fresh produce from the market, and deliver orders to customers. Dad said the van had belonged to Ryan's grandparents, who had owned the shop before them. Ryan loved it. Lots of people stopped to stare at them as they drove around the town, because the van was so special.

Today, to Ryan's surprise, Mrs Bayley packed the boxes of fruit and vegetables into a shiny, new blue van.

'Where's the red van, Mum?' asked Ryan.

'It's at the garage being repaired. They've lent us this new one until it's fixed,' said Mum. 'Actually, that red van is much too old now. Your dad and I think it's time we had a new one.'

Ryan didn't say anything. The blue van smelled new and looked very shiny. But the red one was like an old friend.

Their first stop was Mrs Dawson's house. 'Goodness, what's happened to your lovely red van?' she asked when Mrs Bayley brought her order.

'It's being repaired,' said Ryan's mum. 'So we're using this new one for a while.'

'Well I hope you get it back soon,' said Mrs Dawson. 'You don't see many vans like that nowadays. It's a classic.'

'Well... I suppose so,' said Mrs Bayley. Ryan smiled.

Their next stop was Mr Pandya's.

'Where's your lovely red van?' asked Mr Pandya.

'It's being repaired,' said Mrs Bayley.

'I hope you get it back soon,' said Mr Pandya. 'You don't see many vans like that nowadays. It's a classic.'

'Well... yes,' said Ryan's mum. Ryan smiled.

Wherever they went, it was the same. Everyone asked about the old red van. They all missed it.

Ryan's mum didn't say much on the way home. Ryan could see she was thinking hard.

As they got back to the shop the man from the garage phoned.

'Your van's ready,' he told Mrs Bayley. 'Did you say that you wanted to sell it? I could take it off your hands.'

'Oh no! I don't think we'll sell it after all,' said Mrs Bayley hastily. 'You don't see many vans like that nowadays. It's a classic, isn't it?'

Then she looked at Ryan and winked. 'Want to come with me to pick up the old red van?' she asked.

'You bet!' said Ryan.

Karen King

Early years wishing well: Journeys and transport

The old red van

Personal, social and emotional development

★ Set up a greengrocer role-play area with a till, cardboard-box van, vegetable boxes, writing materials and food. Encourage the children to take turns to be the customer, the shopkeeper and the delivery van driver.

★ Ask grandparents and great-grandparents to talk about how they used to shop and the types of vehicles that they saw as a child.

Communication, language and literacy

★ Make a 'Greengrocer lotto' game by enlarging two copies of the photocopiable sheet on page 89 to A3 size. Colour one copy and laminate it to use as the gameboard, and laminate and cut up the second copy to use as the cards. Play by turning the cards over, and if the child can name the product, they match the card on the gameboard.

★ Play 'Initial-sounds lotto' using the cards and board above, with the child saying the initial sound of the product. To help with letter recognition, word-process a set of lotto cards showing the initial sounds or words.

Mathematical development

★ Use a van-shaped sponge and red and blue paint to print a repeating pattern.

★ From a safe vantage point, look at the different types of delivery vans and lorries that pass your setting. Record the results on a simple tick sheet.

Knowledge and understanding of the world

★ Visit a local transport museum to find out about classic vehicles.

★ Invite the children to make vans with construction toys and to draw them. Ask them to swap vans and become mechanics, taking the models to pieces and trying to rebuild them, following their drawings.

★ Collect wrappers and labels from food and discover which countries the food comes from. Mount the labels next to a map of the world and link each to the corresponding country with wool.

Physical development

★ Practise winking and blinking with the eye action rhyme 'Open, shut them, open, shut them, give a little wink. Open, shut them, open, shut them, blink, blink, blink, blink'.

★ Help the children to wash, peel and chop up vegetables to make vegetable soup. Spoon the cooled soup into bowls for a snack. (Check for any food allergies and dietary requirements.)

Creative development

★ Let the children print with pieces of fruit and vegetables. Add a window mount to make a greengrocer's window display.

★ Look at pictures of Giuseppe Arcimboldo's paintings, such as *Summer*. Help groups of children to make an arrangement of fruit and vegetables. Carefully, fasten them together with wooden skewers and cocktail sticks.

My family are travellers

My name's Maggie. I live with Mum, Dad and my big brother Eddie in two trailers parked on the site. We have a truck and a car, too. We can use the truck and the car to tow the trailers whenever we feel like going to live somewhere else.

I've lived on three different sites. At our last site, a nursery van came every week, with toys and things for children to do. We could borrow jigsaws and books as well.

Several other traveller families live here, so I've lots of friends. Older children, like Eddie, go to the school nearby. He's getting good at reading and reads picture books to me sometimes, but he likes Computer Club and football practice best.

Our horses are called Patch and Queenie. We tether them on the common to roam about and eat grass. Sometimes we ride them. In olden days, most travellers lived in a *vardo*. That's an old-fashioned horse-drawn gypsy caravan. Vardos were covered with painted decorations and looked very pretty.

When our gran was young, her parents moved around a lot and she never went to school. Now, she lives in the trailer next to ours. She can't read, so Eddie reads his school story-books to her. She makes pretty flowers carved out of wood and collects lovely china plates. I like to hear about the different places where she bought them.

Dad collects scrap metal to sort and sell. In summer, he lays tarmac and does other jobs. Eddie rides in the truck with him at weekends, and helps. Sometimes Eddie has to miss school for about a week when we go to a horse fair. We take the trailers, and the horses travel in a friend's horsebox. People come from all over the country to the fairs: some still travel by road in their horse-drawn vardos.

At the fair, people wash their horses in the river, and make them look smart. There are trotting races, with horses pulling sulkies, and galloping races along the lanes. Lots of people have come to buy and sell horses, but I like seeing the goats and rabbits. Mum and Dad buy things at the stalls: new clothes and perhaps some gold jewellery. We meet up with old friends and have a great time. Then it's home to the site, and Eddie goes back to school next day to tell his friends all about it.

Susan Eames

My family are travellers

Personal, social and emotional development

★ Help the children to compare their lives with Maggie's. Place two pictures of a trailer and two pictures of a house in a bag and ask the children, in turn, to take two pictures out. If they match, help the child to suggest something that is the same in their and Maggie's lives. If the pictures are different, encourage them to find a difference between their life and Maggie's.

Communication, language and literacy

★ In small groups, encourage the children to talk about what they would like to do if they could go away for a week. Record the children's thoughts on to tape for the other groups to listen to.
★ Say to the children the traditional rhyme 'Trot, Trot, Trot' from *This Little Puffin…* compiled by Elizabeth Matterson (Puffin Books) and learn it together.

Mathematical development

★ Copy the photocopiable sheet on page 90 for each child. Challenge them to cut out and fit the furniture and items into the vardo, making sure that no items overlap and that none is missed out.
★ Give each child a copy of the photocopiable sheet on page 90. Encourage them to decorate the vardo in repeating patterns using small shape stickers.

Knowledge and understanding of the world

★ Collect different household items made from a wide range of materials. Challenge the children to find different ways of sorting them, for example, by material (metal, plastic), function (cooking, washing) or where they are found (kitchen, lounge).
★ Ask a parent, carer local person to bring in a pony or horse for the children to meet. Encourage them to think of questions to ask beforehand so that they can find out how to look after a horse properly.

Physical development

★ Invite the children to each decorate a paper plate as a souvenir of a local place. Ask them to add a collage design by cutting up pictures, magazines and postcards from the local tourist information centre. Encourage each child to glue these to the centre of their plate, then punch holes along its rim. Provide the children with thin ribbon fastened to a short length of drinking straw for them to thread through the holes.

Creative development

★ Invite the children to make their own vardos to use with small-world people. Make two copies of the photocopiable sheet on page 90 for each child. Cut out the vardos and encourage each child to paint them on both sides. Glue them to either side of a small open box so that the wheels rest on the table.

Early years wishing well: Journeys and transport

Helpful wheels

My big sister, Claire, hurt her foot and couldn't walk. A nurse at the hospital lent us a wheelchair to push her along the corridor to the X-ray Department. Later, the doctor looked at the picture of Claire's foot. There were no broken bones, so she had a special bandage put on it and her foot was soon better. Dad said it was lucky there was a wheelchair at the hospital, because Claire was too heavy to carry far!

My grandpa has a wheelchair because his legs don't work very well. He can walk a few steps, but he mostly goes around in the wheelchair. It has a bicycle bell on it, just for fun, and lots of stickers. He collects stickers and we often bring him new ones. He lets me ring the bicycle bell, but not in the street in case it startles somebody. Grandpa also has a special stair lift in his house, to take him upstairs and downstairs. He leaves his wheelchair next to the bottom step, sits on the chair, presses a button, and up he goes to the top. He lets Claire and me ride on it, too, when we're at his house. We go up to fetch his spectacles, or other things he's forgotten to bring down.

At the shopping centre, people can borrow wheelchairs to ride around the shops. When Grandpa shops at the big supermarket, he uses a special shopping trolley that fastens onto the front of his wheelchair.

In the street, there are slopes where people in wheelchairs can easily get up and down the pavement. Grandpa says it's a bit of a bump for him if there is no slope. That's why my dad made a concrete slope up to Grandpa's front door.

Some wheelchairs have a motor to drive them, but Grandpa pushes the two special pushing wheels round to make his chair move. When we're out with Grandpa, we push so that he can rest.

It isn't just older people like Grandpa who have wheelchairs. My friend Grant lives in the flat next door. He's six, and he's had a wheelchair for a long time. We have races together in the park, me on my scooter, and him in his wheelchair. On the roundabout, we whiz round so fast, we scare our mums!

I'm glad someone invented wheelchairs to help people like Grant and Grandpa.

Susan Eames

Helpful wheels

Personal, social and emotional development

★ Invite local people of different ages, who use a wheelchair, to talk to the children about how wheelchairs help them to get around. Ask them to explain which things are easier to do with a wheelchair and which are difficult.

★ Let the children take turns to sit in a buggy for five minutes while activities carry on around them. Ask them to explain how it felt not being able to get out of the buggy. Could they join in with everything?

Communication, language and literacy

★ Think of words that have 'wheel' in them, for example, waterwheel, wheelie bin and wheelbarrow. Record the children's suggestions on to wheel-shaped pieces of paper.

★ Make a 'sound wheel'. Draw spokes on a disc of card and ask the children to place in each segment a different sticker from a sheet of mixed pictures, for example, farm animals, fruit and transport, and write the initial sound of the item represented next to it.

Mathematical development

★ Make a collection of objects that are circular and suspend them from the spokes of a wheel. Invite the children to bring in circular objects, pictures or photographs for a display.

★ Challenge the children to paint flights of stairs with different numbers of steps. Show them how to start at the bottom of the page with the longest stair. Number the steps when they are dry.

Knowledge and understanding of the world

★ Cover planks of wood with different materials such as sandpaper, carpet and thick plastic, and leave one uncovered. Place one end of a plank on the seat of a low chair and test how quickly a toy wheelchair moves down the slope. Repeat with the other planks and ask the children which they think would be the safest for a wheelchair user.

★ Help groups of children to design and make lifts using construction toys and recyclable materials to carry a small-world person to the top floor of a doll's house. Compare the lifts and how they work.

Physical development

★ Design an obstacle course for the children to move along without using their legs, such as slopes to pull themselves up and planks to slide along on their bodies.

★ Show the children how to bandage a foot and then let them practise on each other.

Creative development

★ Help each child to make a roundabout from a disc of card with a pencil through its centre. Invite them to create patterns on it using brightly-coloured paints. Spin the roundabouts and watch what happens to the colours as they whiz around.

Sabia's new outfit

Sabia needed a new outfit. She was going to a wedding for the first time and her mother wanted her to look beautiful.

She had a surprise for Sabia. When Sabia's Aunt Parminder went to India for her holiday, she chose a new kameez for Sabia. Mum kept it secret, ready for Parminder's wedding day.

Mum took Sabia to her bedroom and took out a parcel from one of the cupboards. Sabia untied the string and unwrapped the new, shining, green kameez. It was decorated with beads and tiny mirrors. Mum told Sabia how it was made in India.

The fabric was woven in a factory, then it was cut and sewn to make into a kameez with the shalwar to match. Then they were taken by lorry to the shops in the city. That's where Aunt Parminder bought them. The lady in the shop folded and wrapped them carefully, and Parminder packed them in her suitcase. Then she went to the airport to fly home.

The kameez and shalwar were flown across many countries before they arrived with Aunt Parminder in England. Then they were driven in a car along the motorway to Parminder's house. Parminder gave them to Sabia's mum to keep until the wedding day.

Sabia loved the shiny, green kameez. As they travelled by car to the wedding, Sabia was thrilled to think that her new outfit had already travelled thousands of miles – all the way from India!

Stevie Ann Wilde

Early years wishing well: Journeys and transport

Sabia's new outfit

Personal, social and emotional development

★ Wrap up a set of parcels each containing an item linked to a wedding, such as an invitation, food pictures and photographs. Play 'Pass the parcel' with the children. After the game, encourage the children to talk about any weddings that they have been to.

★ Discuss with the children how keeping surprises secret is a good secret to keep and will make someone happy. Compare this with secrets that should not be kept, but shared, for example, when they know someone is getting hurt.

Communication, language and literacy

★ Plan and hold a role-play wedding and reception. Ask the children to make invitations and place cards by writing their names with metallic gel pens.

★ Share a selection of stories about weddings, such as *Katie Morag and the Wedding* by Mairi Hedderwick (Bodley Head), and non-fiction books such as *Wedding Days* by Anita Ganeri (Evans).

Mathematical development

★ Draw eleven kameez on to green card, cut them out and number them from 0 to 10. Invite the children to decorate them with ribbons, flat beads and sequins, reading the number and placing the corresponding number of items on to each card.

★ Wrap up three small parcels, each of a different weight. Ask the children to find the lightest and heaviest by holding them. Show them how to check their answers with balance scales.

Knowledge and understanding of the world

★ Invite in parents and carers of different religions to bring in clothing and artefacts associated with marriage ceremonies.

★ Find out about the food, clothing and music in India. Hold a special 'India' day, pretending to be Aunt Parminder looking at the route that she took when she travelled to India, tasting Indian food, dressing up and listening to music.

Physical development

★ Provide clothes, paper, tape and string. Encourage the children to carefully fold the clothes, then practise wrapping them up.

Creative development

★ Provide paint, sponges and different types of paper such as greaseproof, brown and tissue. Invite the children to design their own wrapping paper.

★ Ask each child to paint a picture of Sabia in her new clothes at the wedding. Ask them to mix their own green paint from blue and yellow, and to decorate the outfit with foil and sequins. When the outfits are dry, brush them with PVA glue to make them shiny.

The ro-ro ferry

It was the summer holidays. Pierre and Yvonne were very excited because they were going to France with their mum and dad to see their grandparents.

They were going to travel by car to the Channel Port and then drive on to the ro-ro ferry. They couldn't wait!

Dad said the ship was called a ro-ro ferry because the cars rolled on at one end and rolled off at the other. Pierre and Yvonne thought it was a funny name.

When they arrived at the port they had to wait for their turn to drive on board. Their ship was in the dock. The crewmen were busy preparing it to take everyone on board. Large trucks were also lining up ready for their turn.

At last the gangway was lowered and the trucks drove on. When they were loaded, the cars drove on to the upper cargo deck. Dad had to drive very carefully. A crewman directed him to their space, packing the cars close together. It was difficult to get out and reach the stairway up to the passenger decks. No one was allowed to stay inside the car.

Pierre and Yvonne and their mum and

dad climbed up on to the top deck. They stood by the rails to watch the rest of the cars and passengers come aboard. When they looked up they could see the captain on the bridge of the ship where the controls were. Pierre and Yvonne waved to him, but he was too busy to notice them. He had to make sure that everyone was safely aboard and then to sail the ship to France.

It was a windy day, the family went below to find the snack bar. They were hungry after their drive.

After an enjoyable lunch they went back on deck again and were surprised to see that they had left England behind: they had not even noticed that the ship had sailed.

In spite of the cool wind, they stayed on deck. It was interesting to watch all the different kinds of ships and boats sailing along the English Channel. There were cargo ships, fishing boats, catamarans and yachts with tall sails. They even saw a warship and a huge cruise liner. Pierre and Yvonne waved to the people on the cruise liner and many of them waved back.

Soon it was time to go back to the car and roll off the ferry into France!

Barbara Garrad

Early years wishing well: Journeys and transport

The ro-ro ferry

Personal, social and emotional development

★ Ask the children to bring in photographs of their grandparents. Invite them to talk about where they live, how they get there if they go to visit them and what they like doing with them.

Communication, language and literacy

★ Share stories about boats with the children, such as *Who Sank the Boat?* by Pamela Allen (Puffin Books) or *Mr Gumpy's Outing* by John Burningham (Red Fox).
★ Make a ferry-shaped book. Ask the children to find pictures of boats in old magazines, holiday brochures and on the Internet to stick into the book. Help each child to write or scribe a word or sentence to describe their picture.

Mathematical development

★ Develop the children's understanding of ordinal numbers by asking them to drive vehicles on to a toy ferry or drawing so that 'the car is first and the lorry is second'. Ask the children to line up vehicles, and ask questions such as, 'Which vehicle is third?'.
★ Invite the children to use the model ferries made in 'Creative development' and find out which one will hold the most toy cars. Record the number that each ferry holds on to Post-it notes and stick them on to the corresponding ferries.

Knowledge and understanding of the world

★ Make a display of the different routes and ways to travel across the Channel. Include holiday brochures, pictures and a map showing the English Channel, the United Kingdom and France. Ask the children to bring in a variety of toy boats and trains to add to the display, together with models that they have made.
★ Cover a table with protective covering. Provide a bowl of water and a selection of boats and cars for the children to investigate floating and sinking. Can they make the boats sink? How?

Physical development

★ Encourage the children to make different wave patterns on paper with wax crayons. Show them how to paint over the top with water blue paint, working from left to right.
★ Play 'Ships at sea'. Place large pictures around a ferry-related play area, such as of a café, bridge and car deck. Call out different areas that the children should run to and include instructions such as 'Scrub the decks' or 'Stormy sea' (the children should sway).

Creative development

★ Provide a range of small cardboard boxes cut in half lengthways. Ask the children to make model ferries, add details using straws, tubes and cardboard, paint the models and use them in small-world play.

Early years wishing well: Journeys and transport

How things have changed

When Grandma and Grandpa were little they didn't have a car. Grandma said that very few people had cars and most travelled around on bikes. People went to work on bikes and even the policeman rode around the village on a bike. Grandpa said that there were more bikes than cars in those days. Imagine!

Grandma and Grandpa could travel for miles on their bikes. There wasn't as much traffic on the roads then, so it was much safer. I'm only allowed to ride my bike up and down our road. It's not as much fun.

If they had to go on a really long journey, they went by bus or steam train. The buses all had a driver and a conductor. The conductor came round and sold you a cardboard ticket. He then punched a hole in the ticket with a special machine he wore on a strap over his shoulder. It went 'ping!'.

Many people had a motorbike with a side-car for a passenger to sit in. Grandma's dad had one and Grandma used to ride in the side-car. Her dad did not have to wear a hard helmet, like today. He wore a cap and goggles.

Very few people ever went in an aeroplane. Aeroplanes were much smaller and did not have powerful jet engines. They could not travel as far as the planes today. If someone wanted to go to a country a long way away, they would go by ship. Cruise ships were very large and took a long time to get to the end of their journey. It took days to get to America and weeks to get to Australia. Today it would only take us hours.

Grandpa used to travel on ferry boats. He lived near Liverpool and had to cross the River Mersey every day to go to school. Grandma did not go on a boat until she was grown up and went on holiday to the Isle of Wight.

When they were little, I think Grandma and Grandpa had more fun riding their bikes than I do. But *I* have already had holidays in more countries than they ever dreamed about visiting in their day!

Barbara Garrad

Early years wishing well: Journeys and transport

How things have changed

Personal, social and emotional development

★ Ask parents, carers and grandparents to send in any items, pictures and books for a display based on life when they were growing up. Divide the display into sections on transport, toys, games, food and clothes. Emphasize to the children the need to take care of these items.

Communication, language and literacy

★ Share the poem 'Goodness Gracious' by Margaret Mahy from *Poems for the Very Young* selected from Michael Rosen (Kingfisher), about a grandmother bobbing about in the sea. Encourage the children to think of the adventures that she might have had if she had been picked up by a boat.

★ Write the words 'car', 'bus', 'bike', 'boat' and 'plane' in large lower-case letters on to large sheets of paper. Ask the children to push the toy vehicles along the corresponding words, forming each letter correctly.

Mathematical development

★ Copy the photocopiable sheet on page 91. Use the pictures as a guide to draw large simple outlines of different forms of transport on to card. Help groups of children to measure, mark and carefully saw thin pieces of wooden dowel and beading, then glue them on to the pictures. Measure and add pieces of string for the wheels and rigging.

★ Copy the photocopiable sheet on page 91. Cut out the pictures and sort them by the number of wheels that each form of transport has. Can the children think of examples for numbers that are missing, such as a monocycle for number one, or a lorry for number six?

Knowledge and understanding of the world

★ Show the children a large map and point out America, Australia and the United Kingdom. Talk about how long it takes to get to those countries today compared with fifty years and one hundred years ago. Display the times alongside appropriate pictures.

★ Enlarge a copy of the photocopiable sheet on page 91 to A3 size and cut out the pictures. Ask the children to put the pictures in the correct order starting with the oldest. Compare how each mode of transport has changed over the years.

Physical development

★ Collect or make dressing-up clothes based on what grandparents would have worn as children. Encourage the children to put them on and to try to fasten them by themselves.

Creative development

★ Listen to ferry songs such as *Skye Boat Song* performed by Kenneth McKellar (Decca) and *Ferry Cross the Mersey* by Gerry and the Pacemakers (Castle Pulse), adding a percussion accompaniment.

Early years wishing well: Journeys and transport

Buy a ticket

(Tune: 'Frère Jacques')

1. Buy a tick-et, Buy a tick-et, Plat-form three, Plat-form three,

Climb a-board the train now, Climb a-board the train now, Come with me, Come with me.

2. Get your cases,
Get your cases,
Climb aboard the plane,
Climb aboard the plane,
Leaving runway four now,
Leaving runway four now,
Flying off to Spain,
Flying off to Spain.

3. Pay the driver,
Pay the driver,
On the bus,
On the bus,
Riding into town now,
Riding into town now,
Come with us,
Come with us.

Susan Eames

This is an echo song. Sing the first line and encourage the children to copy you for the second line.

Early years wishing well: Journeys and transport

Buy a ticket

Personal, social and emotional development

★ Make tickets for different activities in the setting, ensuring that there is one for each child. They could be for giving out the snack, tidying up or trying a new activity. Place the tickets in a bag and, each day, sit in a circle and play 'Pass the bag' to music. Help each child to read the ticket that they take when the music stops.

★ Ask parents and carers to send in different types of tickets from transport rides, visits, the dry-cleaner's, car parking and so on, for the children to sort, mount and display.

Communication, language and literacy

★ Make an alphabet train with 26 small boxes as carriages. Ask the children to label each box with a letter of the alphabet and fill it with appropriate items – for example, the 't' box might have a toy train, telephone, ticket and tree.

★ Create tickets from card and help the children to write their names on them. Use them instead of name cards.

Mathematical development

★ Set up a role-play ticket office, station and train. Help the children to make different-priced tickets to buy. Limit the seats on the train and ask questions such as, 'How many tickets have you sold?', 'Is the train full?' and 'How many more tickets can you sell?'.

★ Collect together a range of holiday items of different sizes, such as buckets, clothing, cuddly toys and books. Challenge the children to fill a set of numbered children's suitcases or bags with the correct number of items, so that the case will close.

Knowledge and understanding of the world

★ Look closely at different types of toy buses, planes and trains. Place them into individual fabric bags and pass them around a small group of children. Can they work out and describe which vehicle they are holding?

★ Take the children on a bus to visit a local attraction that has ticket entry. Help the children to buy tickets for both.

Physical development

★ Let the children practise stepping on and off benches and planks, and climbing aboard large play equipment.

Creative development

★ Learn the action song 'The Wheels on the Bus Go Round and Round' from *This Little Puffin...* compiled by Elizabeth Matterson (Puffin Books). Make up verses for a train and plane, for example, 'The wings on the plane are long and wide'.

★ Make banging and shaking instruments from recyclable materials, filling shakers with rice, beans, metal nuts or chains. Use these to add an accompaniment to the song above.

Going in a rocket

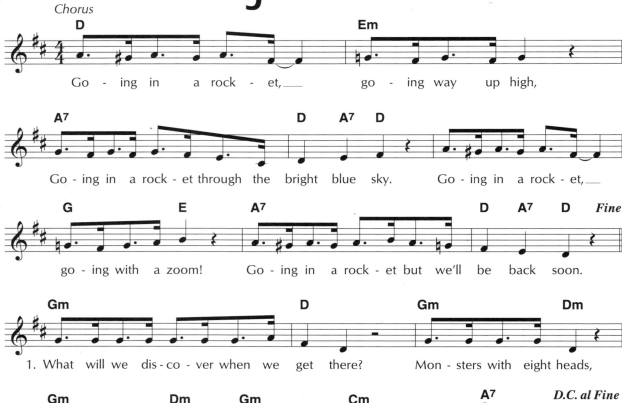

Chorus

Go - ing in a rock - et, ___ go - ing way up high,

Go - ing in a rock - et through the bright blue sky. Go - ing in a rock - et, ___

go - ing with a zoom! Go - ing in a rock - et but we'll be back soon.

1. What will we dis - co - ver when we get there? Mon - sters with eight heads,

Al - iens with ten legs, Shall we go or shall we stay at home? No, we're

2. What will happen if we
   can't get back home?
Lost up there in space,
Lost without a trace,
Shall we go or shall we stay
   at home? No, we're

Chorus

3. Now we've landed safely
   on our planet,
Didn't we go far?
Up among the stars,
Shall we go again to
   somewhere else? Yes, we're

Chorus

Peter Morrell

Early years wishing well: Journeys and transport

Going in a rocket

Personal, social and emotional development

★ Encourage the children to share their feelings about how they might feel if they were lost in space. Talk to them about what to do if they became lost when they were out with their parents or carers.

★ Provide groups of children with a range of pre-cut paper shapes in a variety of colours. Ask them to work together to stick the shapes on to a piece of paper to make a rocket picture. Make sure that every child has contributed. Help the children to display all the rockets on a wall.

Communication, language and literacy

★ Think of words to describe space travel such as 'zoom', 'whiz', 'fly' and so on. List them on a rocket shape.

★ Write as many words as possible to describe space travel on to long thin strips of paper, and ask the children to go over the letters using glitter paint or glitter pens. Display the word strips next to the children's rocket pictures (see 'Personal, social and emotional development').

Mathematical development

★ Cut out monster-shaped bodies from card and laminate them. Number them as appropriate for the children. Ask the children to add play-dough heads and legs to match the number on each body.

★ Draw ten stars on to a sheet of paper and write the numbers 1 to 10, randomly, inside the stars. Invite the children to draw the route that a rocket will take when flying from stars 1 to 10.

Knowledge and understanding of the world

★ Dress a programmable toy, such as a floor robot or car, as an alien or space buggy. Help the children to design and make a planet area complete with craters, rocks and monsters to move the toy through.

Physical development

★ Follow a recipe for cheese straws using ready-made pastry. Help the children to grate the cheese and roll out the pastry. Cut the finished dough into stars, rockets and planets.

★ Pretend to be monsters stomping and waving arms about to the 'Monster Stomp' song in *Game-songs With Prof Dogg's Troupe* chosen by Harriet Powell (A & C Black).

Creative development

★ Invite the children to make 3-D planet landscapes by gluing small cartons, tubs and cylinders (snipped along the end to help them to stick) to thick card. Let the children paint them in bright colours or metallic paints.

★ Make 'pom-pom aliens', threading wool through the cut-out centre of a small disc of card and cutting around the outer edge. Add goggly eyes and pipe-cleaner legs.

Clip clop

F C7 F C B♭ Am B♭ C

1. Clip clop clip-per-ty clop.— Don-key, don-key do not stop.
2. Ca-mel, ca-mel

F C7 F C B♭ C F

Clip clop clip-per-ty clop.— Ri-ding all the way home.

Sing the song about other animals such as pony, oxen, llama and so on.

Clive Barnwell

Early years wishing well: Journeys and transport

Clip clop

Personal, social and emotional development

★ Contact a donkey sanctuary and find out more about the work that they do. Talk with the children about caring for animals and why sanctuaries are needed.

★ Tell the children stories involving a donkey journey, such as Mary travelling to Bethlehem and Jesus riding into Jerusalem.

Communication, language and literacy

★ Copy the photocopiable sheet on page 92 and make camel-shaped booklets for groups of children to write a story about a journey that the animal makes. Scribe a sentence on each page for the children to illustrate.

★ Pass around a pair of staves or coconut shells for each child to clap out the rhythm of their name.

Mathematical development

★ Ask the children to place the animals made in 'Creative development' on a paper 'road' with the donkey first, the camel second and so on to make a wall display.

★ Act out the rhyme on the photocopiable sheet on page 92. Make a line of 12 children, with ten under a sheet as 'humps', and one at either end holding the sheet, wearing either a head mask or a tail depending on where they are standing. As the song counts down, a 'hump' should leave the line until only the head and tail are left.

Knowledge and understanding of the world

★ Compare the work done by the different animals in the song with animals in the United Kingdom, for example, horses on farms. Encourage the children to paint pictures showing the animals at work.

★ Display the children's paintings alongside their writing and any other related material such as artefacts, postcards, models, riding gear and books.

Physical development

★ Encourage each child to make a basic clay animal by rolling and joining together one large and four smaller, fat sausage shapes to make a body and legs. Ask them to add a head and features to create an animal from the song.

★ Invite the children to trot and gallop like the animals in the song. Vary the speed by clapping out the rhythm using percussion instruments, and encourage the children to change direction.

Creative development

★ Draw large outlines of the animals suggested in the song. Ask the children to decorate them using different techniques, including torn paper, fabric collage, sandy paint and snipped wool and string.

★ Collect coconut shells and wooden beaters. Invite the children to experiment making noises and invent their own 'clip-clop' music.

Have you heard?

(Tune: 'Girls and Boys Come Out to Play')

1. Have you heard who's com-ing to-day? There's some-one trav-ell-ing on a sleigh.

Look a-bove the chim-ney tops, It's Christ-mas Eve and he's not far off.

Who can it be? What will he bring? Can you hear peo-ple and an-gels sing?

Long white be-ard and rein-deer too, A sleigh full of pres-ents for me and you. *Can you guess who it is?*

2. Have you heard who's coming to town?
There's someone wearing a lovely crown.
Very soon she will arrive
And wave to people as she goes by.
Let's wave our flags, who can it be?
Will she have time for a chat with me?
Give her flowers and say 'Hello'
Now who can it be – wait I think I know!
Can you guess who it is?

Peter Morrell

Early years wishing well: Journeys and transport

Have you heard?

Personal, social and emotional development

★ Ask parents and carers to send in any books, photographs, artefacts and items that they have about Christmas. Make a display showing how Christmas is celebrated in different homes and cultures.

Communication, language and literacy

★ Enlarge the photocopiable sheet on page 93, which gives instructions on how to make a pop-up puppet. Ask the children to look at the page and decide what it might be for. Give the children time to think, and welcome all their suggestions before reading the page with them.

★ Invite the children to give you possible answers to 'Can you guess who it is?'. What clues did they hear in the song? Ask them who they have seen wearing a crown, for example, Cinderella or a queen.

Mathematical development

★ Make card crowns and number them from 1 to 10. Encourage the children to decorate each with the corresponding number of shapes using sticky-paper shapes or sponge prints – for example, crown 1 will have one shape, crown 2 will have two shapes and so on. When the crowns are dry, let the children add a sequin to each shape.

★ Invite the children to wear the crowns made above and challenge them to arrange themselves in number order while you sing the second verse of the song.

Knowledge and understanding of the world

★ Look in information books for flags from around the world. Count how many different colours the children can find and look at the designs, emblems and patterns.

★ Encourage small groups of children to design and paint flags for the different areas in your setting, and display them in the appropriate places.

Physical development

★ Invite each child to create a handprint angel. Make two silver-paint handprints on to greaseproof paper to create the wings, one white paint handprint for the dress and one pink fist print for the face. When the angel is dry, cut out and stick the face on to a paper body shape, adding the dress and wings so that they are glued at the palm edge only.

Creative development

★ Copy the photocopiable sheet on page 93 on to card for each child. Show the children how to make a simple pop-up puppet by following the instructions on the photocopiable sheet. Invite each child to cut out the shapes and design and make a character based on the song. Provide interesting collage materials such as twigs for antlers, doilies, jewels, fleece and velvet.

Postcards

(Tune: 'I Had a Little Nut Tree')

1. Post-cards tell of tra-vels, Ad-ven-tures near and far, But

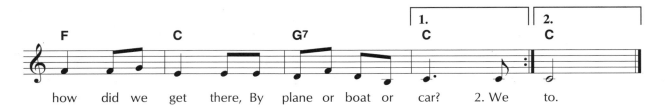

how did we get there, By plane or boat or car? 2. We to.

2. We could go to the seaside
We could go to the zoo,
And postcards will tell you
The places we went to.

Catherine Morrell

Early years wishing well: Journeys and transport

Postcards

Personal, social and emotional development

★ Ask parents and carers to let their children send a postcard to your setting when they visit different places or go on holiday. Display them along a wall for everyone to see.

★ Encourage the children to reflect on places that they have visited. Invite each child to share with the others what they liked or disliked about the place.

Communication, language and literacy

★ Cut out pictures from magazines showing different places, for example, a zoo, beach, farm and space. Display them on a wall. Give each child a copy of the photocopiable sheet on page 94. Ask them to choose one of the places and write a postcard from there.

★ Explain to the children that there is not much space to write on postcards, so messages should be 'short and snappy'. Give them some examples, such as 'Having a lovely time, food good, wish you were here'. Make up some messages together, such as 'Good journey, sun hot, food horrible!'.

Mathematical development

★ Look at a collection of stamps together. Encourage the children to sort them in different ways, for example, by colour, shape, size and numbers shown.

★ Give each child a white self-adhesive label and invite them to design a stamp of their

choice for a postcard. Help them to write the price correctly.

Knowledge and understanding of the world

★ Contact your general post office for videos, computer games and other materials that will help the children to understand the journey that a letter or postcard makes from sender to recipient.

★ Contact a local museum for old postcards and compare these with recent ones.

Physical development

★ Give each child a copy of the postcard on the photocopiable sheet on page 94. Encourage the children to use scissors with different cutting edges to carefully cut out their postcards.

★ Invite the children to cut old postcards into pieces to make jigsaws.

Creative development

★ Make a card copy of the photocopiable sheet on page 94 for each child. Invite them to decorate the front of the postcard by painting, printing patterns or drawing a picture, and then to write a short message and who it is for on the back.

★ Create a 'Holiday hideaway'. Provide simple props such as fabric, chairs, boxes containing clothes, buckets, spades and toy animals, together with a post-box and the materials to make postcards.

Fairground drivers

(Tune: 'This Old Man')

1. Come on Mike! Come on Mike! Time to go, so ride your bike!

Mu - sic's start - ing, Let's be on our way, On this mer - ry - go - round to - day!

2. Come on Jan, come on Jan,
Time to go, so drive your van! *(and so on)*

3. Come on Wayne, come on Wayne,
Time to go, so drive your train! *(and so on)*

4. Come on Gus, come on Gus,
Time to go, so drive your bus! *(and so on)*

> *This song uses the idea of a traditional merry-go-round with various types of transport fixed on to it. Invite the children to sit in a circle and mime the driving actions of each kind of vehicle mentioned in the song.*

Sue Nicholls

Early years wishing well: Journeys and transport

Fairground drivers

Personal, social and emotional development

★ Encourage the children to talk about visiting a fair and what they might see there.

★ Hide items around your setting associated with fairs, such as vehicles from the song, a coconut and pictures of rides. Play some fairground music and encourage the children to look for the items.

Communication, language and literacy

★ Show the children photographs of roundabout rides in information books. Ask small groups of children to make up short 'Guess what I'm riding on?' riddles – for example, a plane might be 'Two round wheels and wings out wide, high in the sky I fly'.

★ Chalk shapes of a bike, van, train and bus on the ground, large enough for the children to stand inside. Sing each verse of the song, tapping a triangle when the name of the vehicle is reached. Ask the children to run to the matching vehicle shape, before singing that verse again.

Mathematical development

★ Ask the children to make a repeating pattern with transport-shaped sponges and paints around the edge of a large paper disc to resemble a roundabout.

★ Talk about roundabouts being a circular shape. Go for a walk to find other circular things around your setting.

Knowledge and understanding of the world

★ Using construction toys based on connecting straws or cogs and wheels, encourage the children to make roundabouts, investigating how to make them turn around.

★ Collect together robust battery-operated tape recorders and music tapes. Encourage the children to play with them to find out how to start and stop the tapes. Provide blank tapes and show the children how to record their own music.

Physical development

★ Use chalk to draw a very large circle on the ground and challenge the children to ride vehicles around it, imagining that they are on a fairground ride and keeping a safe distance from each other.

★ Ask the children to pat and roll out play dough until it is flat, then to drive toy vehicles across it to make different patterns.

Creative development

★ Invite the children to paint pictures of the vehicles mentioned in the riddles made in 'Communication, language and literacy'.

★ Ask the children to decorate large, open-ended cardboard cartons to resemble vans, buses, trains and bikes, adding shoulder straps so that the children can wear them and run around in them. Give the children some chalk and ask them to draw pathways for the drivers to go along.

Going to town

(Tune: 'Yankee Doodle')

1. Bill and Bon - nie went to town, Ri - ding on a po - ny, They

soon found it un - comf - 'ta - ble, The po - ny was all bo - ny.

2. Bill and Bonnie went to town,
Riding on a bike,
They went so fast that the chain fell off
And that they didn't like.

3. Bill and Bonnie went to town,
Riding on a scooter,
They bumped into a busy shopper
They should use a hooter.

4. Bill and Bonnie went to town,
Riding on a bus,
They paid the driver, bought a ticket,
Got there without fuss.

Hazel Priestley-Hobbs

Early years wishing well: Journeys and transport

Going to town

Personal, social and emotional development

★ Make several enlarged copies of the bus, bike and scooter pictures on the photocopiable sheet on page 95. Cut them in half and fasten one half to each child. While singing the song, ask the children to find their other half.

Communication, language and literacy

★ Paint a street-scene background and add the children's paintings and models of transport, buildings and people. Make word cards for the children to match to the scene.
★ Make a copy of the photocopiable sheet on page 95 for each child. Cut out the transport pictures at the bottom of each sheet and ask the children to listen carefully to your instructions to put them in different places, for example, 'Put the people on the zebra crossing near the church' or 'Put the bus on the bridge over the stream'.

Mathematical development

★ Make an enlarged copy of the transport pictures on the photocopiable sheet on page 95. Cut them out and arrange them on the floor. Ask the children to sit next to the one that they use to travel to town, then count the children. Arrange the children as circles, rows and lines and repeat the counting, helping to develop conservation of number.
★ Make four different-sized enlargements of each of the transport pictures on the

photocopiable sheet on page 95. Encourage the children to arrange them in size order.

Knowledge and understanding of the world

★ Provide opportunities for the children to examine a collection of different bikes, tricycles and scooters, discovering similarities and differences.
★ Go on a journey with the children to your local town. Take photographs with a digital camera of the things that you see on the journey. Show the pictures on a computer and ask the children to describe the journey that they went on.

Physical development

★ Invite the children to make a road layout, build bridges and create a town with bricks. Introduce cars and buses for the children to move along the road and under the bridges without knocking them down.
★ Give each child a copy of the photocopiable sheet on page 95 and ask them to make the stream into a railway line by drawing lines from top to bottom.

Creative development

★ Encourage the children to look closely at the different shapes and lines on a bike or scooter, and then to each draw it using a pencil on white paper, or a silver pen on black paper. Mount the pictures and display them with a real bike or scooter, if possible.

Aeroplane, aeroplane

(Tune: Based on 'Twinkle, Twinkle, Little Star')

Ae-ro-plane, Ae-ro-plane in the sky, Ae-ro-plane, Ae-ro-plane fly so high.

Ae-ro-plane, Ae-ro-plane car-ry me, On my jour-ney to the sea.

Ae-ro-plane, Ae-ro-plane in the sky, Ae-ro-plane, Ae-ro-plane fly so high.

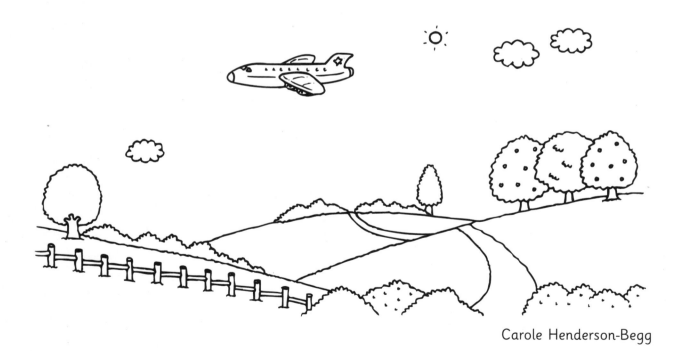

Carole Henderson-Begg

Early years wishing well: Journeys and transport

Aeroplane, aeroplane

Personal, social and emotional development

★ Set up two rows of chairs with an aisle in between as in an aeroplane. Invite the children to take a flight while the 'cabin crew' (adults) serve in-flight snacks to the 'passengers', encouraging good manners.

Communication, language and literacy

★ Sing the song and listen to the rhymes. Write a list of the children's suggestions for other rhyming words to the key words in the song. Make them into silly sentences, for example, 'A tree on the sea'.

★ Create a 'Silly rhymes' book with the sentences made above. Ask the children to draw a picture for each rhyme. Place the book in the book corner for the children to enjoy.

Mathematical development

★ On a large piece of paper, draw a runway and numbered gates to park aircraft. Using numbered toy aircraft, ask the children to fly them down the runway and park them at the correct gates.

★ Introduce ordinal numbers to the activity above, saying, for example, 'Land the red aeroplane first and the blue aeroplane second'.

Knowledge and understanding of the world

★ Talk about travelling in an aeroplane to hot and cold countries. Give the children a basket of assorted clothing and two suitcases. Ask them to sort the clothing into one case for a sunny holiday and the other case for a cold-weather holiday.

★ Make paper aeroplanes from different types of paper such as card, tissue, brown paper and so on.

Physical development

★ Learn the rhyme 'Aeroplanes, Aeroplanes, All in a Row' from *This Little Puffin...* compiled by Elizabeth Matterson (Puffin Books). In a large space, encourage the children to pretend to be aeroplanes flying around by moving their arms.

★ Using a long bench, invite the children to pretend to be aeroplanes taxiing along a runway, arms outstretched as wings, and jumping off safely at the end to represent take-off. Chalk a 'flight path' along the ground for the children to pretend to fly along at different speeds.

Creative development

★ Go outdoors and invite the children to look at the sky, but warn them not to look directly at the sun. Then give them blue, white and black paint to mix their own colours, and encourage them to paint a group sky picture on to a large sheet of paper.

★ Give each child a simple outline of an aeroplane and invite them to decorate it with paint and foil. Place them on the sky painting made above.

Come along with me

Come a-long with me, Come a-long with me. I won-der what we'll see, I

won-der what we'll see Trav-el-ling by bus on a sun-ny day, Trav-el-ling by bus on a

sun-ny day. Bil-ly, what did you see, Bil-ly, what did you see

Trav-el-ling by bus on a sun-ny day, Trav-el-ling by bus on a sun-ny day?

Before starting to sing, decide which children will be involved in all the verses that you intend to sing and invite them to stand at the front of the group.

Wait at the end of the verse while 'Billy' responds by saying, for example, 'I saw a police car'.

Make up other verses by:
changing the form of transport at *
changing the type of weather at **
changing the child's name at ***

Further ideas
Use all forms of road transport on one day, all air or water transport on another day and so on.

Susan Eames

Early years wishing well: Journeys and transport

Come along with me

Personal, social and emotional development

★ Make three lucky-dip boxes, one containing pictures of six vehicles, one containing six weather pictures and the third containing the children's name cards. Before singing the song, ask the children in turn to take one item from each box and to hold them up. These form the basis of the verse and who chooses what is seen. Repeat for each verse until all the children have participated.

Communication, language and literacy

★ Play a sound-recognition game with the children based on what noises they might hear while travelling along. Record different sounds on to a tape and provide picture clues. Alternatively, buy a commercially-produced game. Encourage the children to listen carefully and tell you what the noises are.
★ Share the classic poem 'From a Railway Carriage' by Robert Louis Stevenson from *The Works* chosen by Paul Cookson (Macmillan). Point out the train-like rhythm of the poem and ask the children to listen for the things that are seen.

Mathematical development

★ Make a bus-shaped gameboard. Draw two rows of five windows on to the board and add face stickers to ten counters to represent the people. Using a dice marked with 1 and 2 twice, 0 and a sun, ask the children to roll the dice and add that number of people to the bus until it is full. When a sun is rolled, all the people should get off.
★ Pick a handful of toy buses and ask the children to estimate how many there are before counting them.

Knowledge and understanding of the world

★ Cut out a large bus shape from paper and ask the children to paint it to resemble one from the local bus company. Display the bus on the wall.
★ Take the children on a short walk, then ask each child to paint a picture of something that they saw near your setting. Mount the pictures in a row along the painted bus (see above) as windows. Cover each picture with a card-backed foil flap for the children to lift up and name the view from the window.

Physical development

★ Play 'Follow-my-leader'. Pretend to be different forms of transport, making a wide range of movements with the whole body.

Creative development

★ Make models of a favourite form of transport from recyclable materials.
★ Let the children decorate the inside of a box based on a type of weather, for example, a sunny, wet or winter's day. Arrange the models made in the activity above inside the box and stack them up to make a 3-D display.

Stand and wait

(Tune: 'There Was a Princess Long Ago')

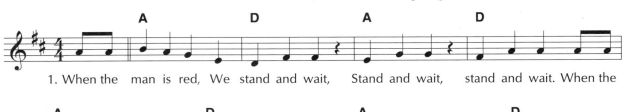

1. When the man is red, We stand and wait, Stand and wait, stand and wait. When the

man is red, We stand and wait For traf - fic fast and slow.

2. When the man is green,
We cross the road,
Cross the road, cross the road,
When the man is green,
We cross the road,
Because it's safe to go.

Susan Eames

Early years wishing well: Journeys and transport

Stand and wait

Personal, social and emotional development

★ Take the children to visit a street in your local area with a pelican crossing and a zebra crossing. Show them how to cross them correctly. Talk about how to cross a road safely when neither are present.

Communication, language and literacy

★ Sing other road-safety songs with the children, for example, 'Stop Says the Red Light' from *This Little Puffin...* compiled by Elizabeth Matterson (Puffin Books).
★ Invite the children to make zigzag books reinforcing how to cross a road, and let them take them home. On separate pages, ask each child to make a red and green sponge-print person and to draw pictures of eyes, ears and heads. Invite them to place the words 'stop', 'danger', 'go', 'safe', 'look', 'listen' and 'think' underneath the appropriate picture.

Mathematical development

★ Make a copy of photocopiable sheet on page 96. Watch traffic going past your setting from a safe place and make a mark in the correct column each time one passes. Use the information to make a simple graph.
★ Watch traffic passing your setting from a safe place and ask the children to comment on whether they think it was fast or slow. Record on to a copy of the photocopiable sheet on page 96, dividing the right-hand section into two columns labelled 'fast' and 'slow'. Ask questions based on the results, such as, 'Were there more fast cars or slow cars?' and 'How many bikes were going fast?'.

Knowledge and understanding of the world

★ Share the book *Look Out on the Road* by Paul Humphrey and Alex Ramsay (*Rainbows* series, Evans) and talk to the group about how to stay safe near roads. Encourage the children to suggest things that they might see when walking along, such as other pedestrians, pushchairs, lorries, buses and shops.

Physical development

★ Play games that involve the children moving fast and slow in different ways such as running, jumping, walking. For example, if you show the children a red man, they should stop moving, stand and wait until they see a green man, when they can move again.

Creative development

★ Sit the children in a circle. Ask one child to walk around the circle playing a percussion instrument either fast or slow, while everyone sings, for example, 'Peter is in the ring, Peter is in the ring, does he play fast or slow? Peter is in the ring'. The child who answers correctly becomes the new player.
★ Make two montages, one of fast things and one of slow things. Ask the children to cut out suitable pictures from old magazines.

One little engine

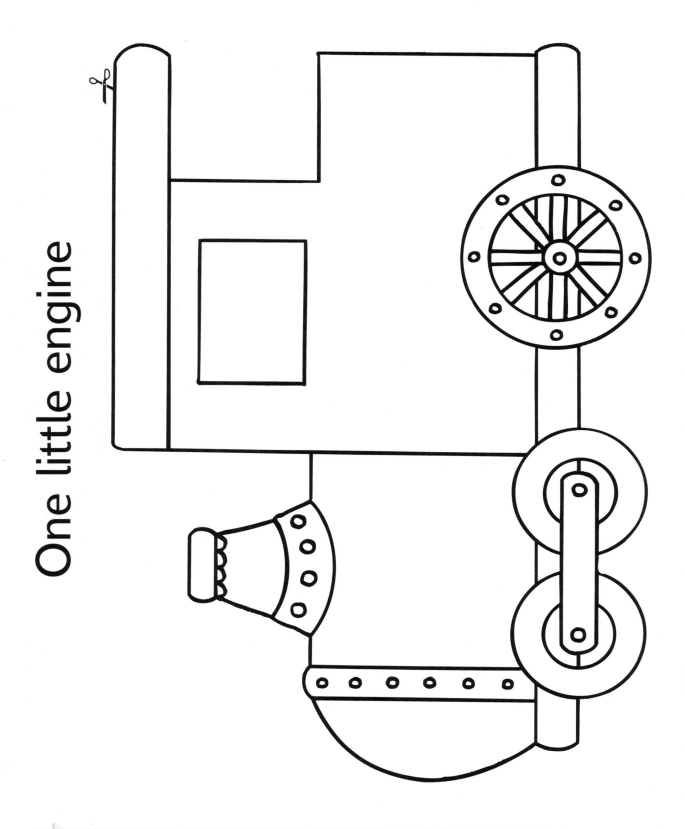

Going on holiday

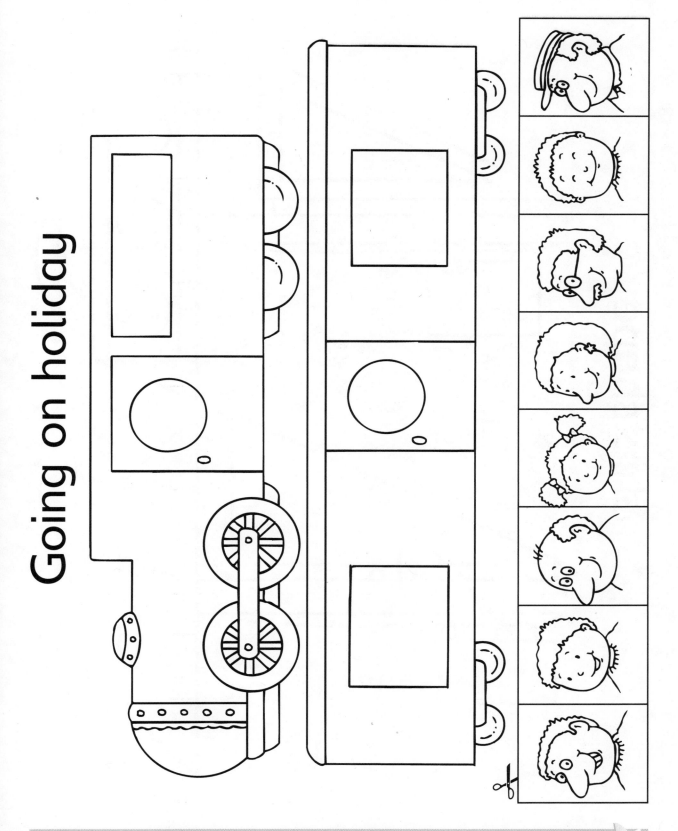

Ship shape

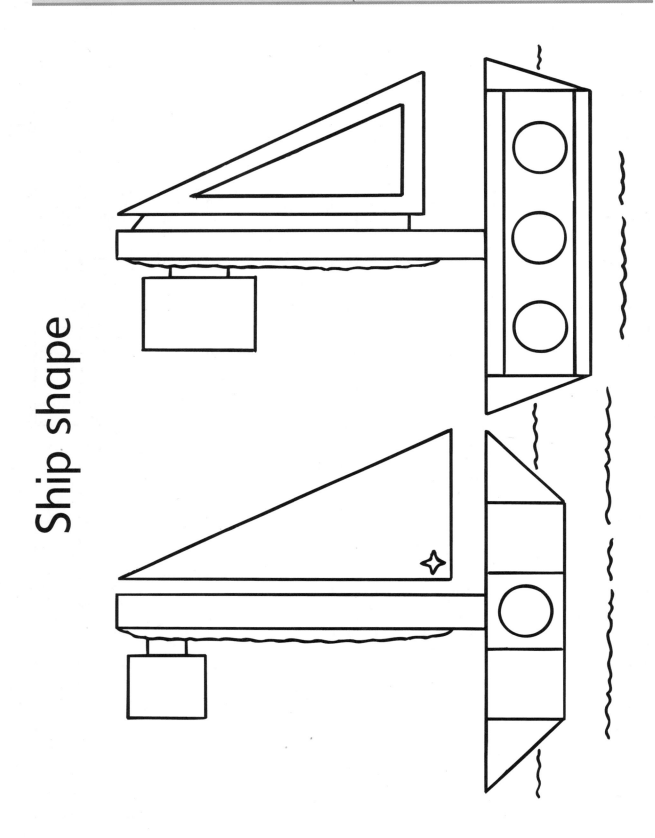

Postbag

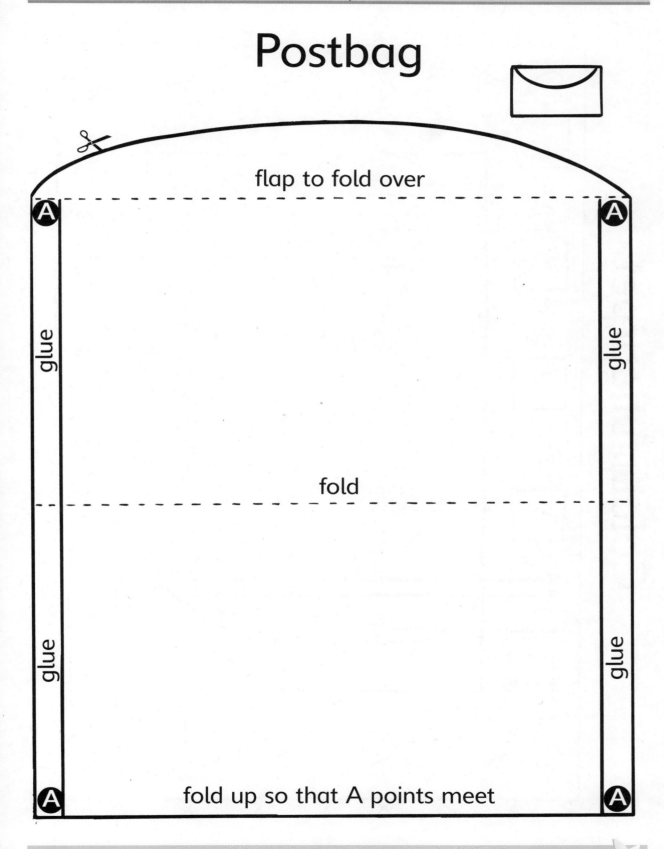

flap to fold over

A   A

glue   glue

fold

glue   glue

A   fold up so that A points meet   A

Colourful carpet

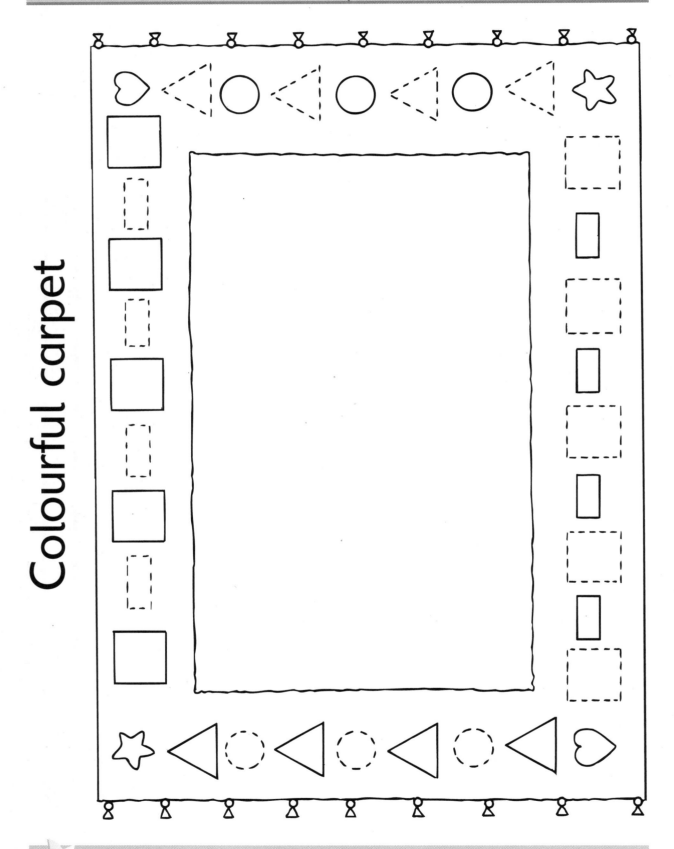

Movement patterns

Balancing bird

Rocket jigsaw

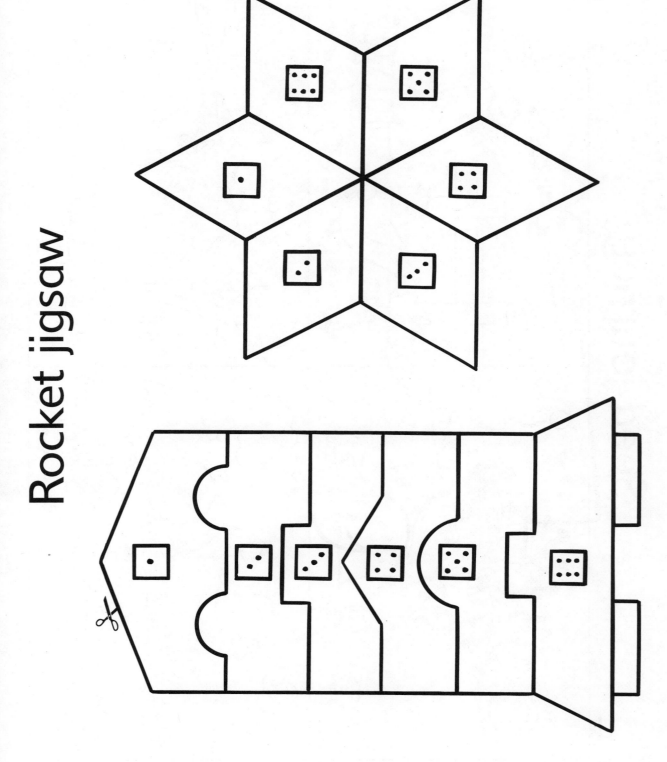

Seed journey

Greengrocer lotto

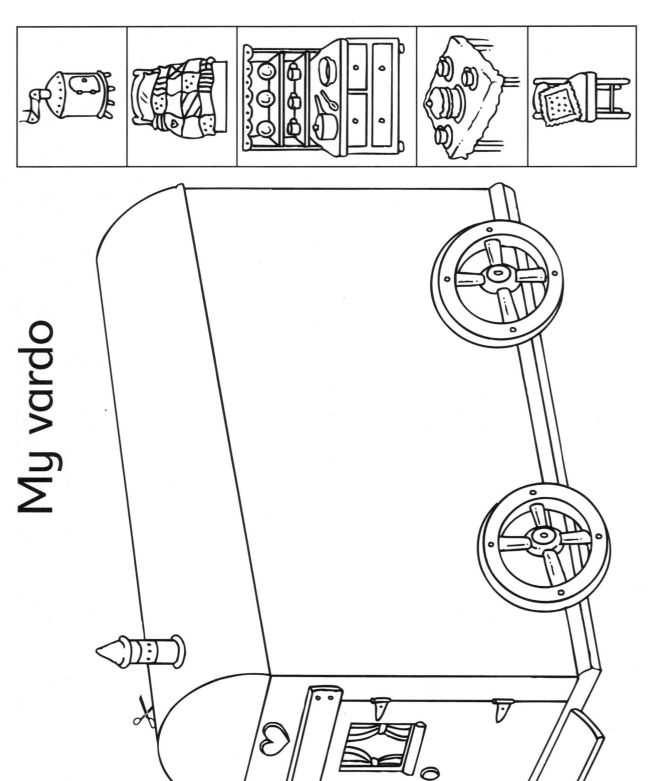

My vardo

Forms of transport

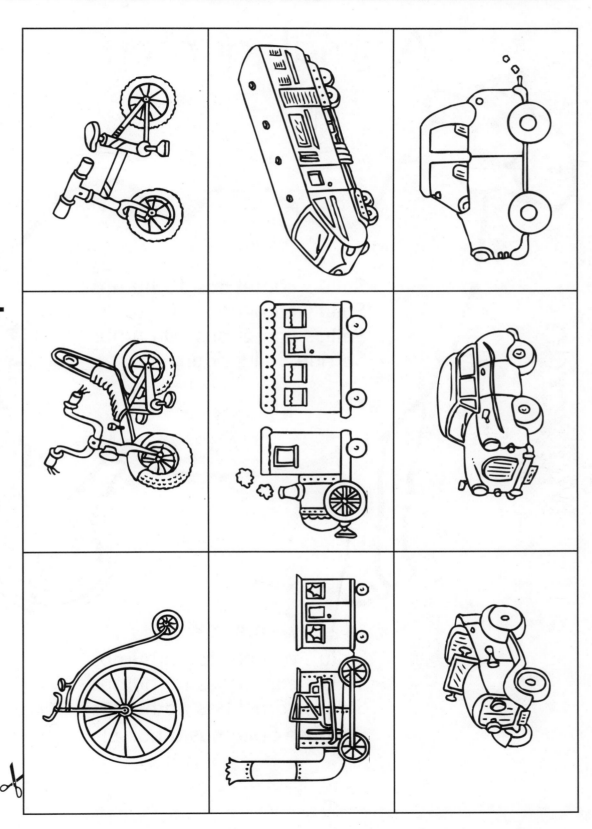

■ SCHOLASTIC

Animal journey

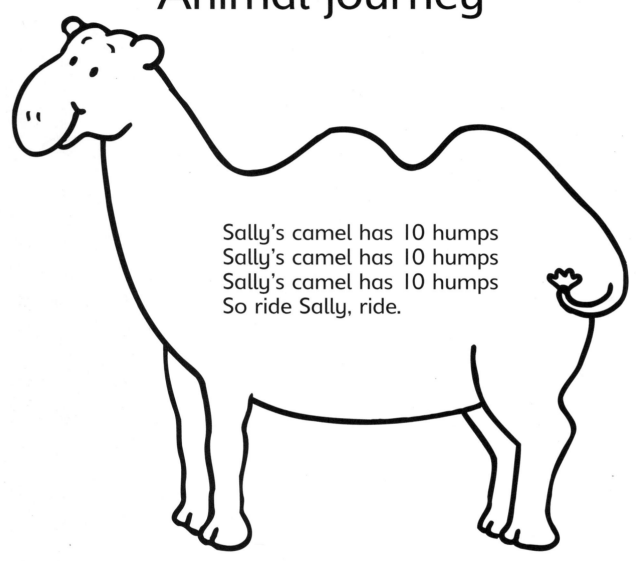

Sally's camel has 10 humps
Sally's camel has 10 humps
Sally's camel has 10 humps
So ride Sally, ride.

(Repeat for 9, 8, 7, 6, 5, 4, 3, 2, 1)
Sally's camel has no humps
Sally's camel has no humps
Sally's camel has no humps
Because Sally has a horse!

Liz Powlay

Pop-up puppet

Put the puppet together

head

body

box

dowel

Decorate the shapes

to make a hat, crown or antlers

to make a face

to make a body

one of each of the card shapes and decorate the box

2cm

3cm

3.5cm

4.5cm

3.5cm

What you need

individual cereal box with a hole

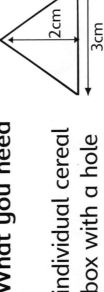

collage materials

glue

tape

25cm

scissors dowel

Design a postcard

Travelling to town

pony

walk

scooter

bike

car

bus

Traffic survey

car	
lorry	
bus	
motor bike	
tractor	
bicycle	
others	

SCHOLASTIC